Also by Darvanni Autonomy

HEAT AND CHEMISTRY

DARVANNI AUTONOMY

TALES
FROM
A
JAIL
CELL

LOCK UP IN AMERICA

AUTONOMY BOOKS

AUTONOMY BOOKS

Autonomy Books
PO Box 22394
Indianapolis, Indiana 46222

Copyrighted© Darvanni Autonomy, 2014

1. Prison in America—Fiction. 2. Lock up—fiction. 3. Prison
drama—fiction. 4. Prison stories—fiction. 5. Incarcerated
minds—fiction.

Illustration by: Saravanan P.

ISBN: 978-1497398788
ISBN: 1497398789

Author's Note

PRINTED IN THE UNITED STATES OF AMERICA

10 9 8 7 6 5 4 3 2 1

Dedicated to the men and women in prison.
Keep faith, stay strong and freedom
will come.

Contents

The Journey through incarceration is more difficult than minds know . . . you have to endure the pain to get to freedom.

INTRODUCTION

Enslaved by the State,
but there's always avenues
to get away.

"Get your ass in there!" the correctional officer yelled, as all six CO's shoved Devon Anderson into his single man cell. He flew into the metal sink and toilet, unable to stop his face from smashing against the wall because his hands were handcuffed behind his back. "Roll'em!" the CO shouted.

Click, click, click, click, click, click, click, click— BOOM! The cell gate shut and locked as the guards chuckled. They found it humorous to see him fly into the wall head first.

The breeze from his body flying blew a stack of papers off his desk and onto the floor. The eight clicks and lock sound echoed through Devon's ears, as the pain throbbed from his cheek bone. He hated that sound. It let him know he was caged like an animal.

"All right, back up to the bars so I can take the hand cuffs off of you," the CO said nonchalant, ready to go sit back down.

He reluctantly complied and as soon as he was unhandcuffed, he turned to face the CO's. "Y'all a bunch of bitches!" Devon bellowed, as he gave a cold stare. The guards just smirked, nodded and walked away. "Just like I thought!" Devon snapped.

The guards were intimidated by him, but acted as if they weren't. *They're cowardly men*, He thought. He couldn't believe he was living in a room smaller than his closet before imprisonment. He began to strip aggressively out of his black gym shorts, white T-shirt, and boxer briefs, then took a bird bath. After he scrubbed the most important parts, he put on some clean boxers and relaxed on his bed.

He was too low in spirit to watch TV because it reminded him too much of what he had been missing, or listen to the radio play over and over the same songs. He enclosed his hands behind his head and stared at the concrete ceiling.

He had to be cell extracted from recreation because he refused to go back to his cell; just as he refused to come to jail by an eight hour standoff with the police because he was innocent; just as he lay there innocent—like a virgin—a reborn again virgin.

I've been stripped of my physical freedom by criminals, he thought. Suddenly, the core door on the range opened. That was an indication someone was about to enter the range. Devon heard unfamiliar voices—some deep—some feminine. His senses went through the roof when he heard a female's voice. It happened to be eight visitors being showed around the prison. They got the pleasure of seeing the animals in their cages.

As they proceeded down the range, they came upon Devon's cell. Devon yelled, "Hey!" then jumped up and rushed to his cell door.

The visitors were frightened and stumbled backwards as if Devon could get to them.

"Don't run away," Devon mumbled, as he eyed the men and women.

The escort stepped up and instructed, "Please don't pay him any mind. That's Mr. Anderson. He's been here for a while. The inmates here in K block—"

As Devon gripped the iron bars of the door, he interrupted, "Yeah! Don't pay me any mind, that's what they always say. But I'm one of the one's whose fighting to get out of prison, while others are fighting to stay in. You made it this far, behind the wall, where anything can happen. Don't run now. Do you really want to know what goes on in here, behind the wall, behind these barb wire fences?"

Most of the visitors nodded while others just stared.

Devon uttered on, "I've been to most of the prisons in this State. They treat us bad—like animals—so we act like animals. As you can see, this is one of the grounds for the living dead. You heard what I said, the living dead. You could be surrounded anytime—attacked or murdered—so you have to stay ready. A lot of these men spend most their lives as slaves, thoughts of freedom they hold all the way to their grave. We live in the past. All our thoughts are old. It gets real lonely in these cells you know. No significant other to hold or whisper too, unless you like punks. And I can't find it to lower my standards to that level. However, I don't know love anymore, but I crave it. All we have to look forward to is—TV, recreation, a phone call—*This*— gas station food for commissary, and if you're lucky—a visit. I spend my time writing. It gives me freedom." He signaled his hand for them to come closer and said, "Take a look in my cell. It's okay. Usually, you'd get killed for

3

looking into someone cell."

A nice looking lady and gentleman approached his cell cautiously and the others kept attentive behind.

Devon took a step back and whispered, "This is my home. Cold isn't it?" He extended his arm out and around to give them a view of his cell. He pointed to reveal as he said, "Not much of anything, a small window just for sunlight because the view is of nothing. Here's my bed where I dream. My little fan for when it gets hot. I keep all my zoom zooms and wham whams in my box right there. On the wall are a few pictures of my favorite models, along with some photos of me having fun in different cities. Them X's on the wall is my homemade calendar were I count down the months instead of the days. And when I want entertainment, I turn on my clear thirteen inch TV. We have basic cable. I made a channel changer for it out of old newspapers and a razor handle. But my highlight of my cell is—my toilet—where I do all my thinking." He chuckled and the visitors giggled along with him. "There's my stinger and hot pot that I cook in. My desk where I do all my reading and writing—"

Out of the blue, the nice looking lady asked, "What are those papers on the floor?"

Devon bent down and picked up a stack of papers and replied, "Oh, these are my short stories about prison. Would you like for me to share a few of them with you?"

She quickly responded, "Yes."

"Well, let me bring you into my world where you have the funniest, most talented and craziest individuals."

TALES

FROM

A

JAIL

CELL

DARVANNI AUTONOMY

VISIT

Stay calm and patient because
some things are hard to swallow.

Keith entered the visiting room, scanned it, locked eyes
with his woman and then smiled warmly at her as he
strolled over to the guard's desk to check in. Prison was a
cold and dark place devoid of any love and warmth.
Weekly visits from his woman, Christy, kept him focused
and connected. He approached their assigned table where
she stood to meet him. He took her into his arms, kissing
her passionately, caressing and groping her softness,
careful not to allow his hands to explore her body too
freely. He knew his every move was being observed not
only by the guards, but also by other nosy visitors. Prison
rules allowed them to kiss and hug at the beginning and
end of each visiting session, and Keith took full advantage
of the rule. He was determined to hold onto his woman as
long as he could, usually force the guard over to their table
to pry them apart. This visit was no different, except for the
fact that their table was right next to the guard's desk,
making their job that much easier. All the guard had to do
to break them apart this time was say, "All right Jones,
that's enough, knock it off and be seated before you get
your visit terminated." They reluctantly released one
another and seated themselves.

As always, the visiting room was crowded, the aroma of microwave popcorn, pizza, and glazed honey buns hovered in the air, coupled with that continual, low rumbling noise emitted by the mixture of many different conversation, laughter, couples arguing, children crying, yelling, and playing. Though the families are crowded in the room together, each table represented a single, private world of its own.

Keith and Christy sat across from one another, Christy, attentive and focused on Keith. Their table was already filled with treats: a pint of chocolate milk, a jumbo glazed honey bun, two sausage and egg croissants, and a bag of barbecue chips for Keith and a diet soda for Christy, who was trying to lose weight and never ate anything during her visit with her man.

Keith spoke first, questioning his woman, "Is everything cool?"

"Yeah baby, everything's fine. I mean, at first I freaked out a little bit because they'd put us so close to the guard's desk, but I still handled business."

"Good. That's my girl." He slipped a couple potato chips from his already opened bag and popped them into his mouth.

"So yeah, like, I figured that being positioned so close to the desk would actually make them less suspicious of us, ya know?"

"See, that's what I like about you, ya feel me? You smart. Know how to use that pretty little head of yours in more ways than one."

Christy blushed. She lived to please her man.

The guard's desk was to his immediate left, about four

feet from their table. In addition to the usual two guards stationed there, there were two others hanging at the desk. Keith might've been nervous, suspecting a trap because of the two extra guards if it weren't for the fact that the two guards assigned to work the visiting room were young, fairly attractive females. The two extra guards were males and Keith was certain they were there to flirt with the other two, especially being that the four of them seemed to be having their own private little party, laughing and giggling, oblivious to their surroundings. The only reason one of the male guards had turned and said anything to Keith earlier when he had been kissing his woman was because, Keith had went too far, kissing and hugging his woman for a full two minutes, showing no signs of stopping anytime soon. The average couple usually did no more than give each other a peck on the lips, and a hug, the whole ritual lasting no more than five to ten seconds tops.

Keith was confident and ready to make his move. He said, "Baby, go and heat my croissant and honey bun up for me, please." He reached for his chips and admired the full figured sway of his woman's ass and hips as she strolled to the microwave. Sticking his hand into the bag, his fingers immediately came into contact with what he had been searching for: a double-balloon wrapped ball of good weed.

He played it off and munched on a few more chips, his plan being to finish the chips, so he could turn the empty bag upside down and pour the ball of weed into his mouth, swallow it, and then throw it up later once he got back to the dorm.

He poured the ball of weed into his mouth at the same moment Christy had returned with his food.

"Here you go baby," she said sweetly, and placed his food before him like a seasoned waitress.

He swallowed the ball and realized too late that it was too big to go down. It got jammed in his windpipe. He was startled, but somehow managed to maintain his composure and not panic—he couldn't afford to. If he had made a scene, the guards would've rushed over and performed the Heimlich maneuver or some shit, and he would've been finished—him and his woman both.

Still, he just sat gagging and fighting a silent battle with the ball lodged in his throat. He couldn't speak or make any kind of gestures for help, nor get any air. His heart raced, his eyes rolled around in their sockets, bloodshot, now revealing altered panic. It was his eyes that warned Christy that something was terribly wrong with her man.

"Baby!?" she said, leaning towards him searching his twisted features. Frightened now, she thought, *Oh my God, he's choking! Choking off the weed*!

Damn, damn, damn, damn, damn! he thought. *I'm about to choke to death—and they gon' lock this bitch up for bringin' me this shit, plus, probably charge her with murder, or some shit. Milk, milk, milk! Try to push the shit down with some milk.*

All Christy could do was watch while her man choked to death. On the one hand she wasn't dumb enough to make a scene by leaping to her feet to assist him, thereby arousing the attention and suspicious of the guards. On the other hand, was the powerful, instinctive urge to help her man. Torn between the two extremes of helplessness and aggressive action, she was paralyzed.

Keith grabbed the carton of chocolate milk, took a big

gulp, and prayed it would dislodge the ball of weed from his throat. The milk didn't budge it, but instead, back splashed and caused him to choke and gag, and chocolate milk to pour from his mouth and nostrils.

One of the guards turned and asked, "You all right Jones?"

Keith calmly tucked his chin into his chest and made a hand gesture signaling to the guard that he was fine. Fortunately, the guard turned and finished conversing with his co-workers.

Christy calmly arose from her seat to get more paper towels.

She handed him some and placed the rest on the table before him then sat back down. "Please, God. Please, please, please, please, PLEASE, God help us through this," she whispered to herself, repeating the prayer over and over to herself while she sat fixated on her man.

Finally, with one last hard effort to swallow, the ball dislodged itself and moved down, unblocking Keith's windpipe, and enabling him to breathe freely and speak.

"Damn!" he said, holding his neck with one hand. "I almost choked to fuckin' death!"

Tears of joy and relief flowed down his and his woman's face. They grasped hands across the table.

"Oh my God, baby, you scared me so bad," Christy said, "I didn't know what to do."

"Shiiiit," he said chuckling, "you did exactly what you were supposed to do—nothin'"

Ten minutes later Keith began to get cold chills and felt completely drain and feverish. He also had a sharp pain in his chest. He was sure it was due to the ball of weed slowly easing down in his esophagus.

He was partly right at least. The ball of weed had indeed gone down, but it wasn't easing down still. Actually, when he had swallowed, it had moved down a quarter of an inch, but lodged itself into the fragile cartilage of his trachea. The precarious position allowed air to flow freely now, but would become stuck again in his windpipe and kill him if it became dislodged. It was simply too big to fit down his esophagus and worse, his body's defense system was treating the foreign object as an invading germ or disease, against which it had no defense. If he didn't somehow get the ball dislodged and out of his body soon, his body would shut down from having expanded all its resources fighting the invader and giving him a fever so high, that he would pass out, slip into a coma and die.

The two decided to end their visit so he could return to the dorm and rest.

Their kiss was brief, but deep; their embrace, long and hard.

It was the middle of July—90 degrees out—but by the time Keith reached his bunk he was exhausted and freezing. He put on a sweat suit and balled up under a thick quilt blanket. Sweat was pouring from his body as he slipped in and out of consciousness.

Suddenly, he arose from his bunk and staggered to the restroom, where he grasped the sink with both hands. He stuck his finger down his throat, and in one hard heave, up came the ball of good weed. Within seconds, he felt rejuvenated. He stood and held the ball in the palm of his hand. His eyes were locked on it as he smiled to himself. It was time to smoke.

Will it ever end
What's that
Slavery
Hell no...Too much money to be made
So everyone's a dollar sign
You got it

MICROWAVE

You never can tell what's
Popping in the microwave

J.P. finally reached the big house, behind the wall, after going through all the complications with going through the Reception Center. He stood in a crowd of men waiting to hear their next destination. He wore an orange jump suit, white T-shirt, boxer shorts, socks, and low-top canvas shoes—Bob Barkers—A.K.A. Jackie Chan's. His uncle told him there would be days like this.

The CO yelled out, "Chapel! A-6! Shank! B-22! Peterson! B–17! . . . " and continued to call out guys cell rooms.

That was him—James Peterson—being told his cage number. He picked up his mat and bed roll and proceeded down the long range to his assigned cell. It was three tiers and he was on the middle one. The human kennel was bright from the lights off the ceiling, but dull in appearance. The paint was chipped from the engraved sayings in the floors, metal railings, bars, and walls.

As he walked down the range, guys of all cultures watched his every step. Their eyes appeared to look for fear, fresh meat or a new lover. He could tell from the distorted visage of characters a lot of monkey stuff goes on in here. *Somebody gonna try me and I'm gonna have to beat they ass*, he thought.

As he entered his cell, he noticed specs of blood from old battles on the wall outside his cell. He glanced around the black hole inmates call home. *This is my new home*, he thought. His stomach turned. It was the worst feeling from a thought he ever felt. He dropped his mat on the metal frame connected to the wall. Suddenly, an older man popped up at his cell entrance. The older man asked in a deep voice, "Hey, you want to use this disinfectant to wipe down your cell?"

J.P. gave a nod as he looked back and said, "Yeah." J.P. extended his hand out as he took a couple steps towards the entrance.

The older man stepped in and handed J.P. the bottle of disinfectant and a rag that was from a cut up towel and said, "Just put it by the door when you're done. I will come by and get it."

"All right."

He walked out and J.P. began to clean his cell. J.P. was new to this, so he wiped down everything in his cell: mat, bed frame, walls around where he had to sleep, sink, and toilet.

There was a loud smack sound then scuffling of tennis shoes. J.P.'s eyes shot towards his cell door. Then he heard several heavy blows and explicit words used. He hurried to his cell door and looked out. There were two men fighting on the first tier. Other men began to break it up because the CO's were coming. Everyone began to scatter and act as if nothing was going on as the CO's barged onto the scene investigating.

A lot of things rushed through J.P.'s mind as he turned

around to finish cleaning. He knew he had to be ready to fight at any giving moment. He assumed, he couldn't let anyone punk him because everyone would think they could do the same, and that would lead to other things: constant fights, extortion, forced sex acts. . . . *Oh my God*! He thought. *I can't let anyone punk me.*

As he made his bed, the same older man popped back up and said, "Hey, Youngsta." J.P. turned to look at him as the older man asked, "Can you take this bag of popcorn to the microwave and pop it for me?" He extended his hand with the bag of popcorn in it.

J.P.'s facial expression turned funny because he didn't know this man and he was looking for a punch line, but there was nothing. J.P. studied his appearance. *He looks pretty healthy to me*, J.P. thought. *A little gray in his bread and hair, but mechanically fine. Was this a set up to walk into an enemy or brawl?* J.P. asked, "What's up? Why you ask me that?"

The older man gave him a crazy look as he hissed and pulled his arm back and then walked out of J.P.'s cell.

J.P. stepped to his cell door, stuck his head out and looked down the range. He saw the older man trudge into another cell. He glared down at that cell for a moment and then scanned around. On the first tier he saw the dayroom, TV, blue chairs, and the microwave. Everyone was socializing, some reenacting the fight that just happened. There weren't any familiar faces that he knew, so he couldn't find any freedom by talking to an old associate. From that, caged bitterness began to eat at his mind. He turned around, took a few steps and fell onto his bed.

His stomach growled. He hadn't been eating that much,

just enough to survive. His appetite was small from the painful thoughts; besides, the food was terrible. He needed to find out when he could order commissary.

He held up his inmate identification card and looked fixedly at his photo and six digit D.O.C. number. *I become a slave to the State*, he thought. From that dark thought, he flung his I.D. to the end of his bed. He rested the back of his hand on his forehand and locked the other one in his palm as he stared at the ceiling thinking about the injustice he received. *I defended myself, so what I beat the guy to death, he attacked me*, he debated in thought.

His thoughts were interrupted—the older man had emerged into his cell and stopped. J.P. quickly raised straight up out of curiosity of what was going on. The older man held his right hand behind his back as if he held a weapon.

J.P. asked in a defensive type of voice, "What's up?" as his hands gripped the end of the metal frame on either sides of his body.

The older man stared at him strangely before he spoke, "Can you go to the microwave and pop this bag of popcorn for me. I brought you one for doing it." He displayed his right hand with the popcorns in it.

J.P. peered at him inquisitively as he slid his feet inside his shoes. His stomach talked again. This time it was a deep growl. He wondered why the older man couldn't go pop it himself. *Was the fight earlier over the microwave?* J.P. thought. *Anyways, this is right on time because I'm hungry.* J.P.'s mind was fixed on food, so he said, "Yeah, I'll go down there and pop it."

He took the popcorn and strolled down to the first tier to

the microwave. The microwave had coffee stains and food caked all over it. He grabbed the rag that was next to the microwave and wiped the inside of it out. He kept an eye on his cell as placed the popcorn in the microwave. He watched the older man disappear off into a cell. J.P. gave a nod to two passing inmates that had their face and body marked up with all sorts of evil tattoos. It seemed everyone was cutting their eyes at him. *Were they sizing me up?* J.P. thought. The vibe made him kind of suspicious. When the popcorns were finished, he headed back to his cell.

The older man abruptly cut into J.P.'s cell and said, "Thanks Youngsta." He reached out as J.P. handed him the bag of popcorn.

"All right, good lookin'," J.P. said, and watched him leave right back out without saying anything.

Formerly, J.P. heard a lot of stories of what goes on in prison and how men tried to manipulate newcomers to be there lover, but was he being targeted. *Oh, what the hell,* J.P. thought, *I'm going to eat this popcorn and if he wants any smoke, he's going to feel the fire.*

Later on that day, J.P. was startled out of his cat nap by what sounded like an army of men fighting. He jumped from his bed and rushed to his cell door and peered out. It was going down right in front of the microwave. About ten guys fighting. He saw men gripping shanks, and some had shanks that looked as lawnmower blades. He glanced at his cell door and tried to slide it shut, but couldn't. His door could only be rolled closed mechanically by the CO. He stared back at the action. *Damn, that guy just got stabbed,* he thought.

There was a loud horn sound and the CO's bombshell the brawl with tear gas. Every fighting inmate scattered accept for the ones that were stabbed up, but there were a few that ran with their cut wounds.

J.P. fell back into his cell from the spreading tear gas. All the cell doors began to roll closed, and whoever was not in their cell was targeted. He sat back on his bed with his T-shirt covering his face coughing. *This shit here is crazy*, he thought, *and this only the beginning*.

They were put on lock down for a few days. While on lock down, J.P. went to the quartermaster and received his required State issued clothes to wear, talk to the counselor, made out his visiting and phone list, went to medical, and worked out the whole time in his cell. He had to wait a few days before his phone list was activated to call anyone. He couldn't wait to be able to call his uncle.

As soon as lock down was over, the older man popped up at J.P.'s cell door bright and early and asked," "Can you warm this up for me?" He had a microwave bowl in his hand with food in it.

Here we go with this shit, J.P. thought, as he stared at him.

The older man spoke, "I brought this pop tart for you."

J.P. was reluctant to speak, "What do I owe you?"

"For what?"

"For the pop tart?"

"I'm giving you this for doing me a favor. You don't owe me anything."

J.P. was knowledgeable from his uncle's talks about the tricks men played by giving a newcomer something then ten times it by what he gave him. He had to make sure.

J.P. took the bowl of food down to the microwave, warmed it up and brought it back to him. He enjoyed the pop tart as he sat on his bed. He didn't have any problem going to the microwave for the older man, but from there on it became an everyday question. Three or four times a day. It got to a point where J.P. started to feel as if he was getting played as a kid or bitch, so he went down to the older man's cell and confronted him and told him he had to start doing that shit himself. The older man was shocked and played timid. He told J.P. he wanted to sit down and have a talk with him and that he will come down to his cell in a minute to have one.

J.P. curious to what he had to say left out the older man's cell and walked back to his own. *Is this guy on some gay shit?* J.P. wondered. *What does he have to say for us to have a sit down and what the fucks he on?*

Finally after a long impatient ten minutes of waiting, the older man appeared at J.P.'s cell. "Knock, knock," the older man said, standing in the doorway. "Can I come in?"

"Yeah," J.P. replied.

As the older man walked in he asked, "Do you mind if I sit on your toilet?"

"Go head. Hold on! You ain't on no gay shit is you?"

"Hell naw! Cause I asked you to go to the microwave for me?"

"You got arms and legs, walk yo' ass down there and do it. Ain't nothing wrong with you. Why can't you go to the microwave?"

"What you think I'm trying to make you my bitch or

something Youngsta?"

J.P. jumped up and stood broadly in the older man's face and said brusquely, "Ain't nobody gonna do that."

It went silent as they sized and stared each other down.

The older man snarled barley moving his lips, "You might have taken me wrong, but I have never been on any gay shit." He took a step back and eyed J.P. with a crazy killer look. His left eye twitched. "I might look funny, but I'm not into any games."

"You don't got to be on no games to pull a fast one."

The older man stepped closer as he began to speak aggressively, "Youngsta, I'm about to tell you something. Don't you fuckin' tell a soooul." He slowly sat on J.P.'s bed and indicated for J.P. to do as well as he eyed him with a senseless expression. J.P. sat down and the older man began to tell his reason, "One night I came home from the bar. I got home earlier than I expected. I walked up stairs to my bedroom planning to lay it down for the night, but before I could reach the door handle. I heard moans. I noticed the moans were coming from my wife. It through me off, I thought she might have been playing with one of her toy's getting ready for me. So I opened the door to sneak a peek and I saw my wife on top of a man riding his—Dick! She killed me inside right then. I eased the door back, went down stairs to my stash, grabbed my three-fifty-seven and quietly snuck back upstairs. Uh, I opened the door without them noticing me opening it, crept up to the bed and was face to face with my wife, but the bitch had her eyes closed. I remember the man looking into my eyes with the fear of God before him as I put my gun to his forehead. I pulled the trigger. Watched his brains hit the

21

pillow. I snatched that bitch up and put her in the head lock, drug her down stairs and choked her to death." He paused, shifted, glanced down at the floor and continued, "I went to the kitchen and grabbed a knife. I attempted to cut her head off, but it didn't work. The knife wasn't sharp enough. I threw the knife and went to the basement to get a saw—my favorite one too. I sawed her head clean off her body . . . but that wasn't good enough. All the shit I've done for her." He started to throw his body around. J.P. began to get nervous, but didn't show it. The older man stood up and expressed with body language, "How much I loved her. She betrayed me in the worst form. I couldn't take it, so I put her head in the microwave and turned it on the highest it would go, and kept resetting it until her head exploded." He gave a deep chuckle and expressed, "So now, every time I see a microwave that experience of seeing that bitches head exploding comes to mind. So I will never use another microwave. And when muthafucka's try to play on my intelligence about the microwave . . . I have the same urge to do them the same way . . . Now . . . do that answer your question?"

J.P. looked up at him but couldn't speak. He was captured in fear, but ready to protect himself at all cost. The older man stood there and glared at J.P. as his left eye twitched.

"Remember what I told you. Don't tell a soul," the older man uttered, and then walked out the cell.

J.P. leaned forward putting his head down in his left palm and massaged his temples. His thoughts were energized by the realization of being trapped—trapped in a place that he couldn't physically escape. There was no telling what his future held in a place filled with so much pain. He couldn't see living life in a cell. He needed to feel some type of freedom, love or support, so the urge to reach out struck him. He jumped up and strolled to the pay phone. He entered his pen number and uncle's phone number and it went through. He felt a since of joy. His uncle answered the phone. J.P. talked rashly in speech. He gave his uncle the run down on everything. He became frantic in thought and told his uncle, "You didn't tell me about no MICROWAVE!"

DARVANNI AUTONOMY

May God be with me as I go
through this painful journey.

Z BLOCK

Where there's smoke,
there's fire.

"9-2-5-6-2-0, 9-1-6-5-1-0, 9-1-0-3-1-4—Move out!" the short over weight correctional officer yelled out as he singled with his right hand forward.

The inmates proceeded in a straight line down the walk of shame, defeat, death and hell. They were leaving intake and heading to their assigned cell block. They carried the minimum: State blanket, two sheets and a hygiene bag. The hallway was bright and cold, an ocean blue, but still dark and spooky. They observed every corner of the tunneled hallway with wonder of where they were being taken to. They all knew from word of mouth they had reached the roughest prison in the State. A lot of men didn't make it out alive from what they've heard. But most of the men had forever and a day, so they were going to see the Penitentiary cemetery anyway. Furthermore, they all had long-term prison sentences as well: fifty-five, seventy, and a hundred and three years.

They came to a stop at this tall metal door that had a sign on it that read—Z BLOCK. Engraved deep in the metal under it read—*The Devils Playground*. They could hear men screaming and yelling at the top of their lungs on the other side of the door.

The CO slid his large skeleton key inside the lock, turned it and slowly opened the old heavy door. He gave a deep chuckle as he held the door opened.

The inmates stepped inside the cell block single file at a pace of a heartbeat. The air was hot, recycled and stale. Instantly, strong smells of sweat, ass, and feet crashed against their noses. They all looked around with screw faces at the large warehouse with five tiers of prisoners acting like wild animals in their cages. Their steps became baby steps as they explored the eyes that stared engrossed. It was a new world—its own world.

The sound of banging metal against metal almost made some of the newcomers heart stop. Burning paper fell from the higher tiers. Caged men on the higher ranges yelled many insulting words and threats at them. Despite all the nightmares they thought it would be like in prison, the reality of it was worst.

"Z-BLOCK MOTHERFUCKER!" Threats came from every direction, "Bitch, I'm going to fuck you straight in your boy puss!"

"You're going to be my little whore!"

"I love that ass baby!"

"I can't wait to get my hands on you!"

But being Rick 9-1-6-5-1-0 wasn't your normal prisoner, he had to say shit back to let them know who they were dealing with. He shouted, "I will kill all you bitches! You don't know who you fuckin' wit. Shut up bitch! I wish you would!"

The sound of laughter echoed. "Ooh yeah! Well, when these gates roll come see me whore!"

As Rick stepped sideways he felt something hit his ball

cap. He stopped and grabbed the brim of his hat. He took it off and found a glob of spit oozing from it. He dropped his bed roll and slammed his hat down. He peered up at the tiers searching for the coward that spit on him. He spotted him laughing standing at his cell bars on the third range, a bald headed white guy covered in colorful tattoos.

The bald headed white guy shouted in a country voice, "Welcome to hell boyyy!" More burning paper slowly fell from above.

Rick bellowed, "You want some smoke!? You'll be the first one I'll kill!" as he pointed up at the bald headed white guy. He snatched up his bed roll, leaving his hat on the ground and trudged to the CO's desk.

The CO gave them their assigned cell numbers. When he told Rick his cell was on the third tier, the look of a killer appeared in his eyes as he gritted his teeth.

Rick maximized his body broadly as he plodded up the stairs to his cell. The guys on the third tier went dead silent when Rick reached the range. When he arrived at his cell bars, a big rat ran across his feet. He jumped back. The rat turned around and looked at him as if this was his place of residence and kept going. He didn't know the men on the range considered that to be their pet rat. That was their only resort of a visit.

He scanned his filthy cell that was closet size. It looked as the last person that was in there before him smeared feces all over the walls. There was a nooses hanging from the ceiling with a piece of paper attached to it. He slowly walked over and read it: *Hang yourself, it's your only way out.*

His cell bars rolled close. The loud lock sound made

Rick slightly jump. At that moment he felt like crying. He had a deep cry on the inside that he wanted to let out. It really began to feel like hell and he was ready to dance with the devil.

Suddenly, the range runner appeared at Rick's cell bars. Rick turned and glared at him. The range runner was short, stocky, and had a fairly dark complexion, he said, "Yo, my brotha, I was told to bring you this because you're going to need it." He slid Rick a long sharp piece of metal with a point on it. The homemade knife stopped at his feet. He looked at it and then stared at the range runner.

"Thanks," Rick uttered barely moving his lips. The range runner then left. He stared at the knife for a moment before picking it up. He gripped the knife in his right hand and at that very moment, he made the decision to use it. He rolled his blanket back, stuffed the knife in it and rolled it back up. He looked around for a clean place to sit, but only found dirt on top of dirt on everything. There were a million dust bunnies under his bed. He smacked the nooses out of anger and when it swung back, he caught it and snatched it down. He paced for an hour before he used wet toilet paper to clean off the bed and sat down. He was waiting for an officer to come by so he could get supplies to clean his cell.

All of a sudden, there was a tornado warning sound as loud as a train's horn that rang out. Somebody screamed out lunch time. The cell doors began to roll opened. Rick hurried and grabbed the knife and stuffed it inside his jump suit and into his boxers. He gradually stepped out his cell and scanned around. He didn't want to get caught by any surprises. Everyone was exiting their cells when, the guy in the cell next to Rick informed, "It's chow time. Stand back by your cell until it closes back."

Rick gave a nod. His mind was on that white guy that spit on him. He knew he had to make an example out of him in front of everybody. *He will never spit on another man again*, Rick thought. *How is he going to spit on a killer like me and expect to live? I'm not never going home, so I might as well get him through there.*

The cell bars rolled back and the CO instructed everyone to go to chow. As they strolled to chow in a single file line, Rick could see the bald headed white guy up a head. Rick stayed position behind different guys to go unnoticed.

The bald headed white guy yelled out to his buddies, "That whore didn't come out. Have you seen him?" as they looked around.

Rick heard what he shouted and ducked behind a big fellow to stay unseen. He was in eyes view and they didn't even know it. The line kept moving through the building and when they landed at the dinning hall's door, the long line came to a halt. They were on standby until the officer commanded for them to go in.

Rick figured this was his best and only time to make his move because he might not get another chance. *No mutha-fucka in this world is going to get away with spitting on me,* he thought. He reached in his jump suit and pulled out the ice pick style knife. He held it close to the side of his leg. His eyes cut around men at the bald headed white guy and his buddies. They were laughing and joking with each other. Rick crouched down and ran towards the front of the line. The line opened like a zipper. Before they knew it, he was right behind his prey. He charged the bald headed guy like a bull and drove the knife through the back of his neck as they fell to the ground. He pulled out the knife and stuck him again and again. Blood squirted out his neck as if it was a fountain. Rick could feel the knife hitting bones. The bald headed guy buddies backed up and yelled for help.

"You dumb bitch! You gonna spit on me. You ain't gonna do it no more," Rick snarled, as he stuck the guy in his neck repeatedly.

There was a loud whistle and then the CO's yelled, "Stand down!" Every prisoner hit the ground, but Rick. He continued to stab the guy. One of the CO's hit Rick in the back of the head with a club stick and knocked him out cold.

When Rick woke up, he was strapped to a bed in the prisoner's medical building with several officers standing by. He overheard the officer telling the nurse that there was one D.O.A. and one restrained. He smiled to himself. *What can they do to a man that's never getting out?* He thought. *What do I have to lose? Not shit.* He slipped back out of consciousness.

Rick was placed on solitary confinement for six months. While in the hole, he lost thirty pounds and went without shaving. He looked rough and rugged. He thought about how he was going to survive when he got out the hole with no family, friends, or money, and far away from home.

When he was let out of solitary, he couldn't keep his eyes open because of the bright lights. They escorted him back to the same cell on the third tier. Only this time, there wasn't any yelling or threats, but so quiet you could hear the guy at the last cell on the long range pissing in his toilet

31

bowl. Rick had earned his reputation to not to be messed with, so he wasn't worried about anyone trying anything. He saw what looked like the same rat wobbling down the range. He shook his head, strolled inside his cell and cleaned. After cleaning, he sat back thinking until he passed out.

The next day different guys were coming to Rick's cell door offering hygiene, food and contraband he could use. That same range runner that gave Rick the knife came to his cell bars and said, "Hey, what's up? I see you back."

"What's up? Yea, I'm back."

"If you need anything let me know. Here's a little care package to get you by." He pushed the laundry bag full of food through the slot for Rick to grab. Rick came over and grabbed the bag. The range runner then said, "I was told to look out for you by your cousin Dave back home."

The range runner turned out to be where Rick was from and went to school with some of his older cousins. It felt good to hear that someone was looking out from back home and that gave Rick something to occupy his mind with. He put Rick up on the prison and how they was in the racist block there because all the other blocks, the white guys were outnumber and a lot of them got tortured . The range runner then said he shall return and left. Rick relaxed back on his bed in thought of his mistakes he made in life.

A few hours went by and Rick heard folding paper and a whoosh of footsteps. He saw a shadow of a person go passed his cell. A folded piece of paper landed inside his cell. He got up to investigate. He tried to look out the bars from each angle to see down the range, but didn't get to see anyone. He picked up the piece of paper and unfolded it. It was a note that read: *You killed one of our brothers. We can't allow you to get away with that. Watch your back.*

That disturbed Rick mentally because he didn't know who just dropped that through the bars and he knew he was playing a deadly game. He instantly thought about getting a blade. Suddenly, the lunch horn went off and seconds later, the cell doors on the range rolled open. The moment of truth was about to come. He began looking around for something he could use as a weapon. He grabbed a bar of State soap, put it in a sock and tied it in a knot, then stuffed it into his boxers. He quickly slid his arms inside the top part of his jump suit and hurried out his cell so he wouldn't get caught by any surprises.

He stood by his cell door and glanced side to side. He looked in the eyes of everyone he came in contact with, studied their appearance and stayed alert of anyone watching him. He began to proceed with everyone to chow. He was cautions all the way there and ate quickly. He made it back to his cell untouched and without any conflict. After the cell bars shut and locked, he settled down in thought of the drama to come.

About an hour later, there were a set of foot prints that stopped at Rick's cell. Rick leaned up in the bed to see who was there. Two men wearing blue hats with holes cut out for eyes as mask, gray sweaters, State pants and boots, were staring right at Rick on his bed. One of them uttered "I'm here to give you a taste of hell."

As Rick arose off the bed, one of the men threw a cup of what smelt and looked as wall paint all over him and his cell. Rick covered and wiped his face. The other man struck a match and threw it in the cell. Instantly, the cell and Rick went a blaze. Rick went crazy jumping all over his cell as he screamed. The men took off running. Rick fell to the floor and rolled around, but the flames gotten worse. Z Block was quiet except for Rick's screams and pleas for help.

The CO's finally came and used a fire extinguisher to put out the fire. But by that time Rick was dead. All you could smell was burning flesh. One of the correctional officers said to a rookie CO, "Welcome to the Devils playground. Z Block."

This is not home
I can be told to pick up
And leave anytime
Because this is not home
They can take me away from
The ones I became close with
Because this not home
I'm told what to do all day long
Because this is not home

RULES OF THE GAME

Along as you know,
you won't mind.

One summer morning Jason was sitting on his bunk in
his cell awaiting a visit. He had been up all night
anticipating seeing his son and daughter for the first time in
five and an half years.

Sitting in his wife beater, boxer shorts and socks pulled
up to his knees, he decided to blow a joint to calm his
nerves. He went in his stash spot and grabbed one out. He
blew O's at his clear plastic thirteen inch TV as he watched
Meet the Browns. He was halfway done smoking when his
cell bars rolled open and the CO yelled, "Young! You have
a visit!"

He finished the joint, splashed on some oil, put his
clothes and shoes on, threw a mint in his mouth and headed
out to his visit. He was patted down thoroughly before he
entered the visiting room. He took his visiting pass to the
CO's desk as he locked eyes with his sister. He gave a nod
to one of his friends visiting his girl as he strolled over to
the small sitting table his family was at. His sister greeted
him with a big hug as his two kids just stood there with a
mystified expression. He took a couple baby steps towards
them, bent over and said, "Hi, I'm your father." He gave
his son a big hug first, brushed his head after he sat him

down, and then picked up his daughter and hugged her as tears eased out his eyes.

Jason and his sister sat down as his kids stood at his lap. His sister watched him questioned and entertained his kids. That made her so happy to finally see her brother with his kids. That's all he talked about whenever he called home. He had left when his son was only six months old and his baby mama was pregnant with their daughter. They didn't waste any time after having their first child to have another one. They were on bad terms so that's why he never got to see them.

He enjoyed their growing minds and got a good laugh from it. His kids wanted to go play with the other kids and toys in the kid's area. He let them go and rapped at his sister. He thanked her for bringing them out.

The kids were running around the visiting room chasing each other when the CO at the desk came to his table and said, "You going to have to put a leash on your kids or I'm going to have to end your visit."

Jason quickly responded, "Leashes is for dogs and they are not dogs."

The officer walked away and mumbled, "That's why certain people shouldn't have kids."

Jason jumped up and was about to snap, but his sister said as she extended her arm, "Jason, let it go."

"Hell naw sis. These muthafucka's think they can talk to you any type of way," he said, and sat down.

"I know. Let's just enjoy the rest of our visit." They continued the visit, but he was still mad as hell.

After the visit was over, he hugged and kissed his family then watched them leave. He couldn't resist the urge to say something to the officer that verbally assaulted him. He walked up to the officer's desk and stated, "Don't let that shit come out your mouth again."

The officer with an expression as he didn't know what Jason was talking about just looked at him without saying a word. Jason strolled away and grumbled, "Dick head mutha fucka."

Jason entered the stripping area to be searched. As he began to take off his clothes, the officer from the visiting room came in and told the other officer, "I'll search him. I think his visitor slipped him something."

Jason instantly said, "Stop lying."

The other officer turned and walked away. The complaining officer glanced at Jason and said, "Bend over and spread your cheeks," as he put on his elastic gloves.

"I refuse. I will squat and cough, but I will not bend and spread them."

"You either comply or I'll do it for you."

"Bring it bitch."

"You people are just so disrespectful," the officer said and smirked.

The pettiness was eating away at Jason and he hauled off and hit the officer across the jaw as he uttered, "Bitch." The officer went flying back into the wall. He reached and grabbed his radio to call for help, but it was no use. Jason punched him again knocking the radio out of his hand. The officer fell to the floor and screamed.

It was on now.

I might as well go all the way, Jason thought. He began to kick and stump the officer's head to the floor. He growled, "Bitch! Bitch. Bitch . . ."

"Hell-elp!" the officer cried.

"Bitch, don't cry now. Take that. Take that."

All of a sudden, several officers rushed into the room and tackled Jason to the ground and handcuffed him. When they pulled Jason to his feet, the officer he beat down hauled off and hit Jason in his mouth and busted his lip.

Jason sucked in his bottom lip and tasted blood. He spit his bloody saliva at the officer and shouted, "You still hit like a bitch!"

The irate officer punched Jason in his stomach which took the wind out of him. Jason gasped as his body went forward. The other officers had to stop the officer from hitting Jason again—not there—not where people could see.

They aggressively rushed him with his arms extended above his head to the elevator and rammed his head into the wall. They continued to apply force pushing his arms up until one of his shoulders was dislocated. They took him straight to lock up—the segregation unit. There, they threw him in a cell and beat him in handcuffs. After they were finished, they took off the handcuffs and left him all bloody and lying on the cold floor. There was no one to call for help but God. He was all alone in a small dark room where life seemed worthless, only had the concrete walls to talk too. It would be hours until he got to see medical. But that's what you get when you let your anger get the best of you.

There has always been an unspoken code. That if you beat down a pig, make sure you do it good because they going to get theirs one way or another. He got nothi· than what he expected.

You signed up for this.
No I didn't.
You took a plea didn't you?
Yeah, but—
Well, you signed your life away.

PRIDE

You can't make rational decisions
when you think your mother's going
to punish you.

A.D was down to his last weekend in a level two prison
from an eighteen month sentence. He was being ware-
housed in a dormitory with one hundred and fifty-six men
and a prison that held twenty-six hundred, far different
from a level three or four prison which had cells.

A.D was awaken by the CO early Friday morning and
instructed to take his personal belongings and gray property
box to "R & R" receiving and releasing for packaging.
Department of Homeland Security Immigration Officials
was coming to get him Monday morning. They were trying
to send his ass back to Africa where he was from. His
green card was in question from his drug conviction. He
arose and gathered himself and took his property and gray
box to R&R.

A.D had spent most of his time playing and smoking
weed to take away the pain. But today, he was fresh out.
His commissary was at an all-time low and his buddies as
well. So the day seemed to drag along. However, there
were a few guys in the dorm that had some for sale.

By the time evening came, A.D began to fiend for the
weed. He started on a marijuana search around the dorm.
He found the dorms bully—Big Sweets to have some

Kush. A.D was skeptical of Big Sweets because he intimidated most men that came through the door and took guys money without giving up anything, in addition to raising prices on things as well. Big Sweets had been doing time for a while and held a rep—not to be fucked wit physically. He could take two or three guys on at one time and found pleasure in choking and smacking guys around as he called them bitches.

A.D continued on with his search because he didn't want to deal with Big Sweets and found the other guys were all out. That left Big Sweets the only one to go to. *Damn!* A.D thought. *But I need some Kush in me before I go crazy.* He didn't socialize himself with Big Sweets so he sent his buddy Mo down to cop for them. A.D gave Mo his last seven dollars in commissary.

Mo in thought of smoking giddily strolled down to cube one. He approached Big Sweets who was sitting on his bed and said, "Hey Big Sweets, let me get two sticks." He handed him the seven dollars of commissary.

Big Sweets calculated the commissary and demanded eight dollars for the two because it was Kush. He went inside his jogging pants and pulled out one joint. He handed it to Mo and said, "Bitch! When you get the other dollar, you can get the other one."

"I-I-I I'll bring the other dollar right back." Mo scrambled away. He came walking towards A.D with a strange look on his face.

A.D asked, "What's up? What's wrong?"

Mo stopped in front of A.D as he showed the joint in his hand and said, "Big Sweets wanted eight dollars for the two and he wants another dollar to get the other stick."

"But its two pen heads for the seven."

"He done raised the price up"

"Man, why you didn't say you was cool? I don't have no other dollar. Take him back his joint."

Mo just stood there. He was scared to take the joint back. He knew he would be called a bunch of bitches if he did. A.D looked at him and said, "Give me the stick. I'll take it back." He snatched the joint out of Mo's hand and walked down to cube one.

A.D pulled up to Big Sweets bunk as he was passing time away with his homeboys. Big Sweets was the loudest one and did most of the entertaining. You could always hear his loud grumbling voice clear across the dorm. A.D slid between two guys to get in front of Big Sweets and said, "Excuse me, Sweets." Everyone went silent as they looked at A.D. "Here's your stick back Mo got from you. I don't have another dollar to give you. Let me get my seven dollars back." He handed Big Sweets the joint.

Big Sweets turned his head back and forth and sat there for about three minutes eyeballing the joint as if he was confused. A.D stood there and wondered what was going through his mind. *What is this fool thinking*, A.D thought. Big Sweets was taken too long, so A.D slowly sat on the end of Big Sweets bed.

Suddenly, Big Sweets shouted, "Get off my bed bitch!" A.D jumped up and stood at attention. His slender physique gave a soft tremble, but he stood his grounds for his money. Big Sweets pulled opened his locker drawer connected to his bed frame and dug through his box full of commissary. He grabbed some items out and put them on the bed. He grabbed a bag of Nacho cheese chips, stood up

and stated, "Here bitch!" as he smacked A.D in the face
with it.

The bag of Nacho chips bounced off A.D's face. Out of
reaction, A.D swung his hand out to block and back handed
Big Sweets in his lips. "Muthafucka!" Big Sweets
bellowed, as he snatched up A.D and put him in the
headlock. A.D looked as an airplane coming in for a
landing the way he held his arms out wide.

A.D began to holler because the grip was getting tighter
around his skull. The surrounding men reacted and tried to
calm down the situation as A.D yelled and staggered
everywhere.

One of Big Sweets homeboys said, "Naw unk. Naw
unk, we will get on his top." Out of the blue, the youngster
uppercutted A.D right in the forehead. A.D screamed and
acted as if he was running in place. Big Sweets let his lock
go. A.D slipped out the headlock, rubbed his forehead and
retreated to his bunk to put on his boots as he heard echoes
of laughter.

After he put on his boots, he rushed back down to cube
one and ran up on the youngster. A.D stuck his chest out
and snapped, "Let's go to the bathroom." The bathroom
was the mutual fighting grounds anytime guys had a
problem with each other. A.D just knew he could take him
because the youngster was only five foot tall, and someone
he thought he could man handle instead of a six foot six
Big Sweets.

Big Sweets walked in between them and pushed A.D
back and said, "I spared you. You have to spare the
youngster."

A.D couldn't spare the youngster, nor let this slid, but

for the time being he just backed away and went to his bunk to wait for the moment to catch the youngster by himself.

The speed knot on his forehead bothered him as the time went by. About two hours later, A.D spotted the youngster from his bunk walking by himself. A.D hurried off his bed and out of his cube. He ran up on the youngster and shouted, "What's up now!?"

The youngster jumped back in defense to get some space and put his hands up. Somebody coached, "Hold on, go in the bathroom!"

The youngster who was really scared without his homeboys avoided going by talking trash and backing away. He went and told Big Sweets what had happen.

Big Sweets, the youngster, and a crowd of men came trudging up to A.D leaning against the wall in front of his cube. Big Sweets stepped up and said as he pointed his hand like a spatula at A.D's face, "You want to fight the youngsta? Y'all can go head in the bathroom and fight, but as soon as you done fighting him, you going to have to fight me."

Right then A.D knew what he had to do, let the youngster go and get Big Sweets together. A.D replied, "I don't want no smoke. I'm cool," and turned away and went to his bunk.

A.D sat on his bed in thought on how he was going to get Big Sweets, *I can wait until Sweets isn't looking and hit him with a lock. I would have to climb over the cube's wall and sneak up behind him and bust his head. But then what if his boys jump me? I have to be able to get away. What the fuck . . . just wait until he goes to sleep and get 'em.* A.D went to sleep on that thought.

The next day, A.D went through the day as if anything
ever happened, but was ready to fight at any moment.
Night time came, well, Sunday morning around four a.m.
and A.D went into the bathroom and sat on the end toilet of
four. He was being partially guarded by a four foot divider.
His friend Pimp strolled in the bathroom to the urinal. A.D
said, "Pimp, what's up?"

"Just draining the weasel. I know you ain't going to let
that slide?"

"Man, I can't go home like this. My mamma gonna say,
'what did you do?' She will kill me if I don't do nothing.
My mamma had a man not a pussy. I'm a man."

"I see your prides in the way."

"Not just my pride, but being a man."

As A.D dropped a lock in a sock and began to put three
more socks over it, Pimp zipped up his zipper and walked
over and saw what A.D was doing. Pimp immediately
commented, "Don't do it on this bracket. Wait until tomorrow because they will let'em kill you in here."

A.D thought about it and made the smart decision to
abort the mission. He went to bed and slept all morning. He
knew tomorrow morning immigration would be there to get
him, but he had to still get Big Sweets. Going through these
last couple days without weed has been mad crazy for A.D,
but his mind was occupied with revenge so he had some
type of substitute.

A.D lounged all day and evening on his bed. He grew
restless and his pride was eating away at him, along with
the thoughts of everyone laughing at him.

It was a little after five a.m. when everybody was
coming back in the dorm from breakfast. Big Sweets didn't
go and was in a deep sleep. A.D was sitting on his bed
peeping out the scene. It wouldn't be long before everyone
went back to sleep, except for the few that watched the
news first thing in the morning. The officers were occupied
and stationed on the other side of the dorm with no
observation of A.D's side.

A.D got his lock in a sock ready to go. He waited until
he saw everyone sleep to creep down to cube one. He
entered the cube at a sneaky pace and shadowed over Big
Sweets to see if he was actually sleep because he slept with
one eye opened. He was calling him a bunch of bitches in
his head as he looked over him. He was ready for action
but nervous at the same time. A picture of his mother came
up in his mind as he thought, *Boy, you bet not come in this
house if you didn't fight back.* Big Sweets bunkie shifted on
the top bunk. A.D eyes shot up at him. He had to remind
himself to hurry up and do what he came to do.

He wrapped the sock two times around his hand and
took a deep breath. He screamed quietly inside as he struck
Big Sweets four times in the head with the lock. The first
two whacks put him in a deeper sleep and the next two
woke him up.

Big Sweets' arms and feet went flying upwards. He
kicked the top bunk and his bunkie flopped up. Big Sweets
roared as he arose.

A.D took off running.

Big Sweets watched A.D. flee as he gathered his focus.
Blood gushed out the four deep gashes over his head and
forehead. He jumped up and went after A.D, but A.D

played a Tom and Jerry type of game with him. It was a good thing for A.D that Big Sweets homeboys was all a sleep, so he only had to deal with him and he wasn't going to let Big Sweets catch him. He jumped over the cube's walls and ran around the dayroom tables.

As Big Sweets stood on the opposite side of the table from A.D, he yelled, "Bitch! That's how you want to leave out."

A.D retorted, "Bitch! That's why you leaking."

The CO's heard the commotion and came from the other side of the dorm. When they saw Big Sweets head covered in blood, they quickly hit their signal button for assistance and came running over to control the situation. Big Sweets saw them and still went after A.D, but couldn't catch him around the tables. He wanted to put his hands around A.D's little throat so bad.

One of the CO's pulled a stun gun out on Big Sweets and told him don't move. Suddenly, CO's rushed through the door to assist. They slammed A.D against the wall and handcuffed him. Big Sweets was handcuffed but kept talking shit. "I'm going to kill you bitch," he grumbled over and over again. A.D laughed as he was being hauled off to the hole. He spent five hours in the hole until Immigration came and got him.

Most of the time it doesn't turn out this way, when a person's pride gets in the way, they usually the ones who end up on the bloody side, but it just so happened to work out this time. They shall meet again.

One thing about prison,
It's sad, but it be some funny
Stuff going in there

SMOKIN' ON KATY

Looking for a girlfriend named Katy
can get you in trouble.

Being locked down in a cell can be disturbing to one individual, but when you have a cell mate you can get along with it can be less distressful, especially when you have something to smoke.

It was just a little after lock down and the CO's had already counted. Will turned on the small boom box radio they had on the floor in the corner with a cardboard box atop it to give it a loud system sound. It made them feel as they were riding in a car with the booming system. The two were as Jake and the fat man in a cell together. Spanky was very short and fat, and Will average height and slender.

Spanky began to dance around in the little space that they had and voiced, "And it's on, and it's on, and it's on. Me and you in the same muthafucken room—woo! We definitely go get lifted up out this bitch and hit the club tonight." He continued to dance.

Will sat on the bottom bunk as he looked at Spanky and shouted, "Go! Go! Go . . . Go Spanky, it's your birthday. We gon'—"

Spanky stop dancing and said, "Naw mufucka, it's not my birthday."

Will laughed and said, "Do the down the way."

"We don't do that where I'm from, we jigulate." He began to jigulate to the music. Will jumped up and started bank head bouncing. Spanky stopped and said, "Man roll the blunt up."

"Don't worry 'bout that. I got that. Get that Foxy ready."

A Foxy was a drink guys made up to make them feel as they were drinking a real drink. It contained kool-aid, coffee, ice, and some type of soda pop, and if they wanted to get real extravagant with it, they would add melted down jolly ranchers. It was a caffeine rush guaranteed to get you going. This was a drink you had to sip slowly to get the full affect.

As Spanky was getting the foxy ready, Will was rolling up blunts of K-2. Will thought about the stories he heard about smoking on Katy and said, "You know muthafucka's be prankin off this shit?"

"Let me prank out damn it. I need it. Anything's better than havin' my mind in here. No mo' pain!"

"People pay the price when they smoke on this. One dude had to pay a hundred thousand after smokin' this for the damages he caused. They say, 'you get the shakes and can't stop. It makes you say and do stuff you normally wouldn't say or do.' And that's only off two blunts. This shit gets you high."

"My guy, that ain't nothin' but some herbs and spices. That's what I want to be doin', the robot, tick, and all the other old school dances."

"Turn that down so they won't be coming by the cell. And put the towel down at the bottom of the door so the smoke won't get out," Will uttered as he pointed at everything.

"You ain't 'bout to work my big ass. You can get yo' little ass off that bed and do this shit."

"I'm rolling the Katy up. Man, put the rug down."

"Fuck it! Let' em smell it, I don't give a fuuuck. It don't show up on a piss test, so they can't write me up. They can come in here all they want."

"Shut up and turn that shit down."

Reluctantly Spanky turned the radio down low and put a rolled up towel at the cell door.

As Will held the blunt up, he said, "You might want to get up in yo' bed for this one. This gonna put you flat on yo' back."

They were backwards living in a cell together because Spanky was shaped as a tomato with legs and slept on the top bunk, and Will, slender with no disabilities, slept on the bottom.

Spanky stepped on Will's bed to attempt to climb on the top bunk and almost slid Will's whole mat off the bed. "Hold the fuck on!" Will shouted.

"What you mean hold the fuck on? Shiddd! This the last night I'm sleepin' on top. You gonna get yo' skinny ass up here. What I look like climbin' up here—"

"Humpty Dumpty."

"Well, Humpty go fall right on yo' ass. I know I bet not roll off this bunk."

"If you did, you would look like a rubber ball bouncing around this bitch, fat MUTHAFUCKA."

"You look like a limp dick with yo' broke ass."

"Man shut up."

This was an everyday thing between the two. Will had

to help Spanky get up top because if he didn't, Spanky couldn't get up there. Getting down was a problem as well. Will would come in the cell sometimes and find Spanky sleeping on the floor.

Spanky demanded, "Now help me get up here!"

Will pushed Spanky by his wide ass to give him a boost up top. Will quickly said, "Muthafucka, don't you fart."

"I hope I do. Shit all over you. Aaaahh!" Spanky yelled, as he pulled himself all the way up top. "Damn! I ain't doin' this shit no mo'. That's a got damn workout. Pass me the foxy and fire the blunt up."

"You in a hurry to kill yo' self, catch yo' breath first," Will said and handed him the foxy.

"You damn right, rather go out right now than die another way."

"I'm going to get you high tonight." Will held the blunt up and then lit it. He blew smoke up at Spanky.

"Pass the mu-fucka!" Spanky exclaimed

"You goin' to get yo' turn." Will blew out smoke and coughed. He took another puff, handed it up to Spanky and got the Foxy in return. He took a sip and turned their TV to the sit-com *House Wives of Atlanta*.

Spanky hit it too hard and began to cough. "Damn . . . damn . . . damn. This some good shit," Spanky sputtered out.

"Yeah I know, these women on here be tripping," Will said and pointed at the TV screen.

"They can trip on me. Hand me a Smooth or a Straight Stuntin Magazine."

"I ain't handing you shit. You ain't gonna be jacking off while you up there. Have me waking up in the middle of the night thinking it's an earthquake goin' on."

After smoking the first blunt, Will gave Spanky another one to fire up. They passed it a few times and Will asked, "You feel it yet?"

"No. Not yet."

"When it hit, you gonna feel it suddenly. I'm starting not to be able to feel my face," Will said, as he rubbed on his face.

"Damn, I think its startin' to kick in on me. I can feel it in my nipples." Spanky thought about what he just said and reverted his words, "Uh, what would you be doin' out there right now?"

"Shiddd, I probably be about to hit the club. Fresh to death, 'bout to see what girl I can pull."

"Yeahhh, I probably be chillin' with a little freak of mines. I miss that shit. Layin' in the bed and she standing up over me dancin'." He handed the blunt back down.

"All the shit we could be doing and we up in this bitch." Will started hallucinating and staring at the wall. He swore to himself that he saw Katy moving her body seductively on the wall. He rubbed the wall and mumbled, "Katy," as if he was rubbing her body.

Spanky heard Will mumbling Katy and looked down to see what Will was talking about. Will had dropped the blunt on the bed. Spanky yelled, "Will! What the hell you doin'? You down there lookin' like the scream mask and shit, feelin' all over the wall."

Will jumped and realized he dropped the blunt. He quickly grabbed it and bushed the ashes off his chest and bed. He replied, "Nothing . . . I thought I saw Katy on the wall"

"Katy my ass, that's that K-2 you smokin'. Watchin' them hoes on house wives got you fucked up. I'm gonna get yo' ass a blow up doll to talk too."

"Naw, just give me Ms. Gunner."

"You like that old piece of ass don't you. Fuck around and catch worms fuckin' that. It's only one bitch that works here I would fuck. And that's Ms. Turner. I would eat her booty, dive right in face first from the back. You can tell she got some good pussy. She stay fresh and smellin' good." The K-2 started to kick in on Spanky. He caressed his chest and gripped his nipples. He was ready to bite into a stripper or eat some food. "Man, my fat ass gettin' hungry. Hit the button and tell'em to send a sack lunch and one of the nurses down to check my temperature. I got my own thermometer. I just can't see it to check it."

Will laughed and said, "When the last time you seen that muthafucka?"

"The last time yo' mamma was holdin' it and said, 'look at it on my lips.'"

"Yeah, okay. You should of told me to hit the button and say, I got a hundred for some head."

"That doesn't sound bad right now. Call the head doctor!"

"What's the best head you ever had?" Will said as he rubbed on the wall.

"The best head?"

"Yeah, the best head you ever had that made you go crazy. Lose control."

"The best head I ever had wasn't from no woman."

"What!" Will shouted, as his eyes bulged out the sockets. This caught him by surprise. *Oh, no, this dude gay,*

Will thought.

"Hold on! Hold on! It may sound crazy but let me tell you the story first. I'm from the country deep down in Indiana. My grandfather had a farm and one day I was out there milkin' the goats. I was lookin' at how those goats suck on them nipples and decided to let the goat suck my dick. I pulled the goat over to the hay stack, pulled my pants down and sat my fat ass down on the hay. That damn goat got a hold of my dick and I went crazy. When I start comin', it thought it was milk and went crazy on my shit. It felt like I was having a seizure. Next thing I know, I couldn't get the damn thang off my dick. Man, I thought it was about to suck my little shit off. I had to hit it in the head with a brick to get it off my dick." Spanky started laughing. Will was in a daze trying to picture it. Spanky put in more words, "One day my little brother caught me gettin' my dick sucked, because after that, I was goin' back on a regular. Well, I told him don't tell nobody and he couldn't get his dick sucked. Couple days later I came out and caught my little brother gettin' his dick sucked. But the craziest thing was he couldn't get the goat off his dick. I tried to help him and couldn't. I even tried my little trick I do to get it off mines. My brother started cryin', so I had to run and get our granddad. He came out talkin' 'bout, 'what y'all doin to my damn goat?' At first he couldn't get it off either. Then he grabbed one ear on the goat and twisted the other one and it let go, then this little muthafucka gonna tell everything. That I got my dick sucked too. My granddad gon' look at me, I'm like, hell, you're the originator, you passed it down. I got my ass beat for that. But that was some of the best head I ever had. I have to take you to

Indiana to get you some."

"Nooo. Nooo. I want some from Katy only." Will was really tripping as he took off his clothes.

"This K-2 got you smokin' on Katy for real. This bitch must be real."

"She is. She's right there on the wall," Will said, and pointed at the wall in front of them. Will stood up, grooved in nothing but his white boxers over to the wall and rubbed all over it as if Katy was standing there.

Spanky bemused asked, "Why you butt-naked?" And then thought, *this K-2 got this dude gettin' freaky with a ghost. I should of never told him about that goat.*

Will started to shake and move unsteady. Little did Spanky know Will was prankin out. He began to move his arms and feet as a zombie. Spanky thought Will was doing some type of dance and said, "Oooh shit! The thriller." Then quoted a snippet of Vincent Price verse off the song Thriller, "The funk of forty thousand years in grizzly ghouls of every tomb are closing in to fill your doom. And though you fight to stay alive, your body starts to shiverrrr. For no mere mortal can resist the evil of the thrilla." Spanky laughed evilly, hit the thriller beat with his mouth and moved his body as a zombie. *I need some more of that* shit, Spanky thought. *I'm tryin' to get like this dude.*

Will glared at Spanky as he moved like a robot and said with a crooked mouth, "I'm about to die. For real . . . I'm about to die."

"Ooh, shit!" Spanky shouted, but was stuck on the top bunk. He shifted around in panic to figure out how he was going to get down safely. His little fat feet dangled back and forth as he looked as a rocking egg on the ledge.

"Help . . . I'm about to die." Will grabbed his chest. Spanky realized it had gotten serious and built the Courage to jump down. He screamed as he tumbled down. When he hit his feet, he knocked the TV off the stand, rolled forward as he hit his head and bowling balled Will like a pin. Will smacked the wall face first and fell backwards over Spanky's body. Spanky had knocked them both out and the position they landed in did not look right.

The CO walked pass and saw them on the floor. First, he had to take a mental picture because his next thought was the two put him in the mind of a limp dick lying across a scrotum sack. He conducted a search of the cell after getting them down to medical and found the K-2. They received write ups that may put their job line at risk, and a ten dollar hospital bill, onto top of a broken TV. It's a price to pay when you smokin' on Katy.

L.I.F.E.

L.I.F.E. and what's the meaning of it
This incarceration takes away everything from it
As I sit in this darken cell
I have no understanding of it
Because everything I see is pain to me
Surrounded by cold things
Crime bricks, a metal toilet and sink
The steel door that traps my freedom
Allowing me only to think
My desk . . . even my blankets are cold
And when that steel door rolls open
Giving me more limited space to move around
All I see is cold individuals lost like me
Having no understanding of L.I.F.E.
Does that mean I'm cold just like thee
Mean mugs, no smiles, just frowns, that's all I see
And when I see a smile
It's somebody trying to get over on me
Damn . . .
I'm stuck in here forever
So what is L.I.F.E.

23 AND 1

The system has its own ways of
disciplining bad boys.

"Aaaaahhh, fuck! He's trying to break my arm. Ah, my shoulder, he just broke my fuckin' shoulder," Stone screamed and groaned, as he was being escorted and tossed into a van by correctional officers to be transported to an super maximum prison, where he would be on twenty-three hour lock down and allowed one hour out his cell.

The lower level prison he was at, the guards were too disrespectful and he could not take it, so he did what his anger told him to do—thrash a Sergeant.

His shoulder wasn't really broken. He said that so they would lighten up on the abuse. He was surrounded by blood thirsty CO's breathing down his neck as the van took off. One of the guards sitting behind Stone, shoved him hard in the back of the head and grumbled, "You want to put your hands on officers, huh." Stone flew forward onto a guards lap. The guard instantly snatched him up and back into the seat.

Stone had already been banged up, but severely battered a few of them before they gotten him. He felt as a prisoner of war or much more of a slave. The handcuffs and leg irons were cutting off his circulation making the ride much longer, uncomfortable, and painful.

They pulled up to the castles of hell that were heavily guarded and fortified by sharp steal. Stone was pushed off the van and onto the concrete. He groaned and frowned. His wrist and ankles felt as they were just cut off. Two of the transporting guards picked him up by his arms and proceeded forward at a fast pace, forcing Stone to take quick short painful steps. The leg irons were cutting at his flesh. He stumbled and almost fell, but they didn't care, they held him up and kept going.

They reached the intake desk and stopped. Stone stood there grimacing in pain. One of the intake officers asked, "Special delivery, huh?"

The transporting officer replied, "Real special. Hard to handle, sign right here and you can have him." He placed some papers on top of a large yellow envelope on the desk and said, "Take care of him for us."

"No, problem." He then looked at Stone and asked, "A tough ass are you? We'll fix that." Stone didn't respond, but just glared into his eyes.

He was brought into an intake cell and stripped. He had to go through the procedures: open his mouth, stick his tongue out, hold his arms out wide, flip his hands around, lift his testicles, turn around and raise one foot at a time, squat then cough. He was given a pair of boxers, T-shirt and a jumper. He was escorted in shackles to a one man cell in the disciplinary unit. His mat and bed roll was already in there waiting.

Stone sat on his bed and examined his bruises. His ankles were cut to the flesh and tender. They hurt worse than the bruises from the beating he took. His mind was too gone to make his bed. He looked around as he relaxed back and used the bed roll for a pillow. He slowly dozed off.

A few hours had gone past when suddenly, the bean hole slammed open and the CO yelled, "Wake up! Slop time!"

Stone was shook out his sleep. He lay there and stared at the door for a while. He was slow to get up because his body was sore. He stood at the steel door and peered out the small triangle shaped window. He couldn't see anything, but heard the food cart wheels getting louder as the cart got closer. The CO rolled up with the food cart and dropped a tray on the cuff board. Stone grabbed his tray and examined it. He looked out the cuff board at the other trays and noticed his tray was short food as the CO prepared his cup of juice. Stone yelled, "My tray short!"

The CO glanced in the triangle shaped window and said, "Your tray is not short," as he placed the cup of juice down.

It was the last meal of the day and Stone didn't get to eat lunch because he was being transported and the guards weren't going to honor providing him with a meal. Stone said aggressively, "My dessert is not on here." He was missing his cake with icing.

"Fuck it."

Stone snapped, "Fuck you bitch!"

"I got something for your ass. You want to talk shit. I'm going to starve you, teach you a lesson. I'm not the one to be fucked with." The guard slammed the slot closed and walked away.

Stone backed away with his tray and sat on his hard mat. *They're real hard behind closed doors,* he thought. *CO's always want to play tough when they know you can't*

*get to them, coward ass bitches. That's why that Sergeant
got the business.*

He ate the little food that was on the tray and sat back
until the guard came to pick up the trays. He slid the tray
back through the slot without saying a word to the guard.
He turned off his cell light and did a few sets of pushups to
blow off some stem before he went to sleep.

The next morning, the guard came to the door and
slammed the slot opened. "Chow!" the CO yelled.

Light headed, Stone stumbled to the bean hole to get his
food. He peered through the small window at the same
guard from yesterday. *Oh shit, here's this Muthafucka,*
Stone thought.

The CO glared at Stone through the window then turned
and spit in his food. He sat the tray in the bean hole and
said, "Here you go."

Stone just stood there and thought, *I ain't eating that.*
He didn't touch the food. He knew from talking shit that
came with it. He lay back down and went to sleep.

Lunch time came around. The same guard brought the
food to Stone's door. He made sure Stone saw him spit in
his food again and sat it down.

Stone bellowed, "You gonna keep spitting in my food?"

"Starve," he said, and trudged off.

Stone sat there starving like crazy thinking what he was
going to do. He pushed the cold water button on the sink
and the water came out brown. He let the water run for a
while to see if it was going to clear up, but it didn't. He
said fuck it to himself and drank plenty water to try to
please his stomach, but it held no substance that his body

needed. There were a couple of old books in his cell on the desk. He picked them up and began to read them to try to keep the hunger off his mind.

Dinner time slowly rolled around. Stone stood at the door peeping out the window waiting for the guard to get to his door with the food. The cart's wheels were as music to his ears as it proceeded closer.

There he is again the same guard, Stone thought. He took a couple of steps back from the door. The bean hole opened loudly. Stone stood there and watched. The CO peered in the darken cell and made eye contact. The guard said, "I told you I was going to starve your ass. You're going to learn who to talk shit to and who not." He took a big hulk and spit in his food again. He sat the tray in the chuck hole, gave an evil grin and walked away.

Instantly, Stone wanted to kill his ass. He could feel his temperature rise. However, his body was getting weak from not eating. He took the tray, sat down and examined it. The saliva was only on a partial of the food. He thought about how hungry he was and how much he wanted to satisfy his hunger. *Fuck it, I can just scrape the spit off and eat what's under it*, he reasoned. He took his fork and picked at the food. He removed the parts he thought the spit was on and then scooped a fork full to eat, but his stomach turned in disgust. His self-esteem wouldn't allow him to eat it no matter how hungry he was. *There's no telling where it all landed at*, he thought. He sat the tray back in the slot. *I will just wait to another CO come by and tell him I'm not being fed*, he thought as he sat back down.

The guard grabbed the tray and the light that was shown

through the door slot vanished with the sound of the cuff board being slammed.

Stone stomach growled viciously. The rumbles echoed through his ears and off the cold walls. He began to get a hunger headache. He got up and drank some more water. He told himself, *if I don't think about it, I won't be hungry*. He sat down on the stool at the desk and stared fixedly at the cream walls. All he could think about was breakfast and the wait for another CO to come pass his cell. He counted how many bricks were in his cell to pass time 374 1/2. He heard different prisoner's voices yelling out their cell door and just listened.

Shifts for the officers had changed and a new one came pass to count. Stone beat on the door to get his attention. The CO peeped in the small window at Stone.

Stone urgently said with his hands pressed on the door, "Man, I haven't eaten in two days. They haven't been feeding me. I need some fooood."

The CO glanced at Stone and replied, "Don't we all," and walked away.

Stone banged on the door and yelled, "I want to make a phone call!" He collapsed to the cold floor and kicked the door a few times. He felt his only hope was gone. The coldness was soothing to his body, so he grabbed his pillow and stayed lying on the floor. Everything played in his mind on how he came to this point in his life, and he asked himself, if God was really real. He eventually dozed off. Morning came and the food slot slammed open. Stone rolled over and staggered to his feet. There he was like a scary movie, that same CO he wanted to kill. He could hear him spitting in his food. This time he didn't even touch the tray, but left it in the slot. He just knew it would be a matter of time before they found him dead on the floor. He wanted to write what happened down so his family would know. He yelled out the door slot that he wanted to make a phone call and write a letter, but he did not have any writing material to do so.

The CO grabbed the tray out the slot and slammed the cuff board. Stone called out mentally to God, praying he heard him. He wished he had the strength to bust through the brick walls as he smacked the wall with his hand. He felt so weak that his vision was blinking in and out. His stomach didn't growl anymore, it just made a thud sound. He sprawled across the floor and just waited for death to come.

Lunch time slowly arrived and the same officer appeared again. The thud sound of the slot being slammed open hurt Stone's ears. He strained to see through the slot at the guard from the floor. He was so weak that he crawled to the door and pulled himself up. Stone uttered, "Hey man, I learned my lesson."

The guard looked through the window at Stone and said, "Dude, fuck that, apologize."

"I'm sorry for—"

"No, no, fuck that. Get on your knees and tell me you're sorry."

"Are you for real?"

"Get on your fuckin knees and tell me you're sorry."

Stone thought about it and slowly bowed to one knee as he shook his head. He was starving. In his mind he had to do it to get what he wanted. He fixed his lips to apologize and suddenly burst up and grumbled loudly, "Fuck you! I ain't getting on shit!"

Stone and the guard glared eye to eye through the small window. The officer could tell he wasn't going to bow down and needed to protect his job, so he slowly slid the tray through the bean hole without spitting on it. Stone quickly grabbed the tray and sat down and devoured it. He could feel his body coming alive as he gulfed down the food. He retrieved the cup of juice the guard put in the slot and took it to the head.

After chow, another officer came and called out shower time. Stone grabbed his small white towel, little bar of Bob Barker soap, shower shoes, and stood by the door.

The bean hole was opened and a mask landed on the cuff board. The guard voiced, "Put that on." Stone put the mask on his face. It was to prevent inmates from spitting on the guards. "Wrap this around your waste," the guard instructed, as he put a chain through the slot. Stone put the chain around his waist. He backed up to the door slot and the guard handcuffed each of his hands to the sides of him, then attached a dog leash to the chain on his waist and instructed Stone to go lie down on his bed. Inmates couldn't go anywhere without being shackled and hand-cuffed and two guards as escorts. The officers came in and secured the leg irons around his ankles. They pulled him up and escorted him to the shower. They walked slowly behind him as one held on to the leash. If Stone made any move, all the guard had to do was pull the leash and it would sweep him off his feet. The bad part about it, he had to take the chains off and then put them right back on when he was finished.

The shower was very small, a tin can that had three rubber strips across the floor. Stone hit the shower button to turn on the water. On contact, he jumped out the way because the water was extremely hot. "Got damn!" he uttered. He ripped his towel to make a wash cloth. He stood to the side and poked his rag in the water. It was too hot to even stand under and steam arose thickly. There was no way for him to control the water temperature. He quickly soaped up and rinsed off. He hit the button to turn off the shower water, but it was controlled by a timer and wouldn't shut off. He yelled for the guards that he was done, but he didn't get a response. The steam was be-coming annoying. He waited for a few minutes and then banged on the shower walls and yelled for the CO's, but it didn't do any good because nobody came. Little did he know, he was getting his hour out his cell. They left him in there for an hour in a half. He was mad but happy at the same time when they finally came

Back in his cell, he had just learned he could only write a letter if he received mail. They would give him thirty minutes to write one and come back to pick up the rubber pencil and letter. He was told he will receive a phone call tomorrow when he goes to recreation.

Stone was mentally breaking down and in there you didn't get to see anyone. He had to remind himself—*be strong, the more you weaken your mind, the more you'll self-destruct.* He wanted to converse with the other guys through the door, but he stayed to himself.

Stone received his next meal and was happy to eat. All he could do was lie down and be still to not burn any calories.

The next morning they called recreation for Stone.
"You have an hour out," one of the guards said, as they escorted him to recreation. He was placed in a room by himself with a basketball hoop. The roof was missing to give fresh air and sun light. He went to the pay phone on the wall and called his mother, but she didn't answer. Then he tried to call his girlfriend and she didn't answer. It was too early and everyone was at work. Recreation was the only time he got to use the phone, and if his family's time was offset from that then he was shit out of luck. He shot the ball for a few minutes and began to look around.

Suddenly there was a bang on the door. It caught Stone by surprise. He moved to the door. There was another knock. Stone said, "Yeah!"

There was a convict on the other side of the door that voiced, "Hey, what's up? What are you in here for?"

"Nothing." Stone was bemused by the question and wondered who this guy was.

"It got to be something series, you in super max." They got to talking more and learned they were from the same city. There was a crack in the door that able them to see each other. Stone peeked through the crack to get a look at him. He had a light complexion, nappy curly hair, seemed to be in his mid-forties, and had one gold tooth in the front of his mouth. He smiled at Stone. He asked Stone if he had anything. Stone let him know he just had the clothes on his back. He asked Stone if he wanted some coffee, but Stone didn't drink it. The guy told him it was a bargaining tool to get what you wanted on your range. He let him know how much he could make off of it and what they will be willing to do, due to the fact they wasn't allowed to order food off commissary on the disciplinary unit—strictly hygiene.

Stone took the coffee and went back to his cell and got to talking to the convicts on the range. They was hype about hearing Stone had coffee and would do anything for a cup of coffee. They began to offer everything that they had: stamps, law books, trays of food, and would even have their people send money. To get the coffee to the other cells, they had to link what they called a—Cadillac—to each other. It was a long string with something thin and heavy on the end so it would go far when they slung it out from under the door. Stone was happy he had received some law books so he could work on his case to gain his freedom back.

Every time Stone went to recreation, this guy would give him coffee. Stone began to think he was a cool dude. One day he told Stone how he murdered a correctional officer in another prison. He stabbed him seventeen times and stabbed the other officer who tried to help eight times. He slid Stone the report under the door to prove it. He had already been down twenty-two years. He was never allowed to be in population again. He had to die alone.

He began telling Stone how the front office messed with his mail all the time and how they would go through his mail and wouldn't give it to him. He asked Stone if he could have some case laws sent in his name. Stone responded, let me think about it.

The next day he brought it up again. Stone told him it was cool, he didn't see any harm in it because he was working on doing his appeal as well. The guy comforted the situation by saying, they were going to send one in his name to and they should get them at the same time.

Stone was getting to know voices on the range from slanging coffee. He heard an unfamiliar voice rapping a song. He listened closely and thought it sounded familiar. Then he heard him say a neighborhood where Stone was from. Stone stretched out on the floor and called out for the guy rapping. He stopped rapping and answered. Stone asked his name. He discovered it was his homeboy all along. Instantly they were excited. They hadn't seen each other in a long while. They yelled out under the door at each other all night until their chest and stomachs were numb and hurting from lying on the cold floor.

The next couple of days at recreation, Stone and the guy didn't go out at the same time. Stone spent his time working out, shooting ball, and trying to contact someone on the phone. Out of anger from not being able to reach someone, he slammed the receiver, took a few steps and looked up at the sky to fly away. Only if he had wings, he could physically soar away, but it was only his mind that actually floated away. His recreational time was limited, so he had to go away, back to his cage. His body was getting old, but his mind was still set at a young age. He never hurt so badly in his attire life. Every day it was a dying pain that stabbed him like a sharp knife. It had him living unhealthy while trying to educate himself. Sometimes when he lay down it felt as he was about to take his last breath. He woke up caged, restricted to his freedom. He was free, but not free as he wanted to be. Only freedom he got was spiritually and mentally. They even took away his freedom of speech. At least that's what they actions showed. He studied law books to try to gain back his freedom though.

And even though he's caged, they couldn't take away his overall freedom.

The following day at recreation, the guy asked Stone did he receive that package yet. Stone responded—negative. For the next couple of recreations, he would ask the same. It threw a red flag up at Stone. *If he hadn't received his package, why he think I received mines*, Stone thought.

The next morning, the counselor came to Stone's door and dropped off a big legal package. Stone grabbed it and sat down. He wondered what was really in there, so he opened it. It was a stack of transcripts. He flicked through the pages and found two pages stuck together. He slid them out and pealed them apart. He discovered a half ounce of weed, some matches, and rolling papers.

Damn, this dude tried to set me up like this, Stone thought. He rushed to the door to see if the CO's were coming. He thought about flushing it real fast, but waited. Everything began to play in his head—how he was stringing him along—how everything lead to this point— even the paperwork to implant fear into him. He under-estimated Stone intelligence. Stone began to add it up in his mind, *all the coffee that he had gave me to survive had got me back right, so I'm obligated to give him something.* He was still mad he used him as a pawn.

Stone stood up on his toilet and yelled through the vent for the guy. He stayed on the range behind him and their vents were connected. The guy came to the vent and Stone yelled out, "The rabbit caught the fox!" Stone was insinuating the guy being the fox the whole time chasing Stone the rabbit and it turned around.

The guy didn't understand the meaning of what Stone was trying to say until the next day they came out to recreation and Stone expressed he knew everything that he did from day one. Stone slid half of the package through the door and demanded four hundred dollars for the rest.

The guy replied, "You going to make me pay for my own shit. It was a mix up. I was supposed to get that one. You were supposed to get the other one."

"Man cut the games. You know what the fuck you did. If you want this, pay the money or I'm going to flush this shit."

"Hold on, don't flush it. I will shoot you some money."

Days went past and he tried to talk Stone out of the weed, but it didn't work. Stone started to sell it up and down the range. He knew if dude ever got to see him, he would try to kill him, but on 23 and 1, you don't get to see anyone.

INTERMISSION

Are you entertained?

Devon removed his eyes from the paper and onto the visitors. He asked, "Kind of crazy, huh?"

The nice looking lady was the first to respond, "I liked it."

Others began to chime in, "Yeah, their some good stories."

"I like the microwave," one said way in the back.

A woman standing in the middle expressed, "I thought that guy was going to die on the visit."

"That goat head took me through a loop," the gentleman said up front. Everyone laughed.

The nice looking lady astonished, "The CO spitting in his food was disgusting." Then put her finger in her mouth as if she was choking herself to puke.

Devon examined the nice looking lady in her tightly fitted blue jeans and green casual shirt that showed a nice amount of cleavage. She was aware of his wandering eyes. She asked, "Do you have any more?"

"I have plenty of stories. Do you have time to hear any more?"

All the visitors looked at the tour guide in approval to listen to more stories. The pressure was put on him and he didn't want to break the excitement the visitors were receiving, so he said, "Yes, you can read another one. But don't make it too long. We have to get going."

Devon committed, "Well now, I get to tell you some more." The nice looking lady smiled. Devon shuffled his papers around and began.

LETTER

Much deeper than
family pain.

I'm confined to a world behind four walls, where nobody writes or accepts collect calls. So called friends don't even think to send a dime. I guess it's true what they say, out of sight out of mind.

In your mind would you trade places with me, then you'd see how cold and lonely four walls could be. I dream at night of faraway places, but only awaken to see the same changing faces.

Often I sleep and wake up alarmed, fearing that my friends or loved ones might've been harmed. Just dreams I admit as I come to my senses, and look out my window at these barbed wire fences.

I get up, get dressed and go on with my day. When it's time for mail call, none for me they say. Not a letter, a note, or even a card, when nobody writes it makes my time kinda hard.

Y'all really don't know what a letter could mean, until you've been where I've been and seen what I've seen. To you it may not mean much, but to me it means a bunch. It doesn't matter though, because until you've been where I've been and seen what I've seen, you'll never know what a letter could mean.

Forever struggling . . . one day it might get better. Psych, who I'm kidding . . . probably when I die.

He signed his name at the bottom of the letter—Phillip, then mumbled, "This is to the world." He enclosed it in an envelope and addressed it to Obama at the White House. It was his indirect message of how such a society prays on the oppressed. He had no one to call or write, let alone money to eat commissary or buy extra clothing. The State only provided eighteen dollars a month for State pay and he depended on that.

He sat at his desk in his gray jogging pants, white T-shirt, and black sandals. He grabbed his wooden handle brush next to his papers and grazed his waves. He then put on his wave cap in thought of lying down to sleep or at least faking at it. His small five-seven body frame began to call for something to eat. He rubbed his stomach.

He arose and slid the envelope under his cell door for the CO to pick up then looked out his cell door window one last time. He turned and glanced at his cellmate in disgust that was resting under the covers watching TV on the bottom bunk. *This muthafucka up here looking weird in a bitch*, Phillip thought.

He grabbed his bowl of food off the desk that he brought back from the dining hall and climbed on the top bunk. He noticed his Cellmate watching the discovery channel as always. *Out of all the things to watch on cable TV at night, he's watching the discovery channel*, Phillip thought. He grumbled to himself while he ate slowly. He had a foul taste for the world or any old friends. It had been years since he heard from anyone, so he had no care or desire to talk to anyone or go back home. *I'm just sitting here by myself, might as well stay by myself*, he thought. This is what prison caused—coldness of the heart. He could tell who his real friends were.

Suddenly, Phillip's bunkie turned off the TV. He did this every night at eleven. He made no attempt to ask Phillip if he wanted to watch it because in his mind, he was treating him as a kid. Phillip paid him no attention, for he knew his cellmate was institutionalized. *Don't nobody care about that old box TV you got from the 80's*, Phillip thought, *muthafucka's got flat screens.*

After Phillip was done eating, he jumped down and washed his bowl. He placed the plastic container in his cubic area and then sat on the toilet to pass gas. His bunkie Stanley had let it be known when Phillip first moved in, if he had to pass gas during lock down to sit on the toilet and flush each time he farted—it was out of respect. Phillip eyes casted over at Stanley, he caught Stanley mysteriously staring at him then looking away. Phillip hurried and flushed two times then got back on his rack.

As soon as Phillip climbed up, Stanley stood and shook his white boxers from between his thighs. Every night Stanley would drip water under the toilet and sharpen his knife on the floor. His sixty year sentence had his mind gone. He was forty-four years of age and had been down since he was seventeen, but you couldn't tell he was forty-four because he didn't age and his face was young as a baby's. He was clean, neat and controlling, and wore his identification card faithfully. His five digit D.O.C. number represented how long he had been down—everyone else had six digits. Phillip wasn't sure if Stanley liked boys or not and knew he murdered to get his sentence, so he played possum every night to avoid confrontation and kept an eye on him. An institutionalized man with sixty years in a cell

at night wasn't to be trusted—and it was frightening to
Phillip.

The sound of sanding filled the silence.

Kneeling, Stanley lifted up and put his hand with the
knife in it on the edge of Phillip's bed right in front of
Phillip's face. Phillip peering out his barely opened eyes
slowly rose.

Stanley stated in an angry voice, "Feel this. Touch the
tip to see if I need to sharpen it some more."

What! Phillip thought. Phillip frowned at him then
stared at the sharp steel. It wasn't anything as seeing a
knife and you didn't have one. The thought of having to
battle against it flooded his mind. He was already
outweighed by a hundred pounds and the only possible
thing that could save him—was far away—the little red
button on the intercom by the door. The guards barely did
rounds making it easy to leave someone begging for their
life. At that moment, Phillip wanted to run to the door and
scream for the guards to get out of the cell. He thought,
when I leave out just refuse to come back in to get moved.

Phillip cautiously touched the tip and answered, "It's
sharp, but you need to sharpen it some more because it got
a curve on one side of it."

Stanley pulled the knife back and backed away. Everything was serious to him—every word, every stare. He
glared at Phillip and snarled, "I take this everywhere I go . .
. never leave the cell without it." He went back to
sharpening his knife.

It was the top of the morning and Phillip barely got any
shut eye last night. The opening of his eyes was filled with

reminisce of Stanley's knife. His ears gained conscious of the movement of convicts outside his door going on about their day. Stanley's box TV was on. *He's not gone this morning*, Phillip thought.

He moved off the covers and jumped down. He really didn't like looking at Stanley but he took a glimpse at his bed. What he glimpsed made him do a double take—a young white man in Stanley's bed reaching to turn the TV.

Eye-opening, Phillip quickly asked, "What you doing?"

The white guy had the look of a man transforming to a woman. He replied as if there wasn't any problem, "Stanley said I can come lay in his bed and watch TV." He turned his head and went back to watching TV.

I definitely got to get out of here now before mutha-fucka's think I'm gay, Phillip thought. *I knew this dude was gay.* He shook his head and got himself together and left out for morning recreation.

When Phillip returned, Stanley was sitting on his bed watching TV. The white guy was gone. As Phillip washed his hands he asked, "What's up with dude in your bed this morning?"

"I don't fuck around. I be extorting them white boys."

"Oh, okay," he said sarcastic.

"Mind your business." Stanley jumped up and shoved Phillip into the wall grabbing him by his collar. With his defiant stare Stanley squeezed out, "And you'll be okay."

Phillip didn't say a word, just shook his head—yes. He knew Stanley had that knife. Stanley let his grip go and slowly backed away. Phillip stepped to the end of their beds, took off his shoes and jumped in his bed. He relaxed back in thought of how to move out the cell.

Later on that day, the CO's came to the cell door and demanded Stanley to back up to the door slot and cuff up. They instructed Phillip to stand against the wall. Stanley grumbled to Phillip, "Pack my shit, make sure I get everything." They came in and took Stanley away. Phillip didn't know earlier Stanley tried to rape one of the new white guys that arrived at the facility, but word would spread quickly and he would know within a matter of minutes. He packed Stanley's stuff and turned it over to the CO's.

An hour later, Phillip had moved his mat down to the bottom bunk and was lounging back when, a piece of paper slid under his door. He looked at the paper then at the cell door window. There was a hallway porter standing there holding a dust mop. Phillip got up and grabbed the folded piece of paper and peered out the door window. The hallway porter stated, "That's from Nova," and walked away.

Phillip stepped back unfolding the paper and found two sheets of toilet paper written on. He read it:

> *If you were stuck inside a volcano and was calling up for help and somebody kept throwing you tennis balls for messages instead of rope, how would you feel?*
>
> *Nova*

Nova was Phillip's friend that was in segregation—the place known to the prisoners as dead lock. He had been in there for a year now, and had written all of his letters on toilet paper. Phillip knew he had to get something down to

Nova from his message. He told Nova for a while he was going to send something, but didn't. The reason for lack of money and the things he scrounged up, he needed.

When the doors popped for dinner, he headed down to his white buddy Richie's cell in a different building. On the way he ran into Freaky T—a big muscle bound booty bandit. "Phillip, what's up?" Freaky T addressed, as he stuck his hand out for Phillip to grip.

Phillip froze in fright then reached out and gripped Freaky T's hand. "What's up?"

Freaky T initiated a hug with the hand shake. When they bumped chest, Freaky T's hand softly trailed down Phillip's spine.

What the hell! Phillip thought, *was that gay?* He quickly pulled away and said, "All right man, I got to get going."

"Don't trip and fall on your way." He stood and stared at Phillip's backside until he disappeared.

Phillip cantered inside a different building and to Richie's cell. Richie's cell door was cracked open. Phillip knocked twice.

Richie was sitting on his bed fixing his radio, he yelled, "Come on!" Phillip entered as his eyes widen from the looks of Richie's cell. It was loaded with everything the prison had to offer. Richie was first to speak, "Look what the wind blew in. What's up brother?" He arose.

"John Cena looking . . . what's up!?" They greeted with a hug and a slap on the back.

"What's been going on?" Richie asked.

"Nothing much, still at the same cell, but, my celly went to the hole today," Phillip replied and smiled.

"Crazy Stanley?"

"Yeah."

"Man, I know it's hard being in a cell with that guy. Let's hope you don't get another one like him. I'm glad I have a cool bunkie. Are you still working recycling?"

"Yeah, but no. I don't care going 'cause they take all my money for State pay."

"Man that's crazy. I remember you telling me that. You need anything?"

"Sure, I'm on the bottom, plus, I have to send Nova down some stuff. I can't leave him hanging."

"I got some cigarettes you can send him so he can get everything that he need. You straight on food?"

Phillip glanced around the cell at the commissary piled high and said, "You don't have too much do you? And what's that smelling good?"

"I just made this gumbo, you want to taste it?"

"Yeah."

They both moved to the desk. Phillip glanced at the picture of him and Richie on the desk that had the liger and lion written under it. He touched it. Richie asked, "You remember that?"

"Yeah, I remember that picture."

Richie opened the food container, grabbed a fork and handed it to Phillip. He tried the gumbo.

Phillip's taste buds went crazy and he exclaimed, "Wow! This here is gooood. Man, I can't wait to get out and get some real food."

"Get you some more." Richie pointed at the food. As Phillip took more bites, Richie informed, "You never know when we might go on lock down, and them things last six months or more. No ordering commissary, no phone calls, shower every three days, just have to be prepared for it. Oh, I forgot to tell you, my mom's haven't been doing well. She's been in and out of the hospital. So my mind has been up and down. And she has my son at the house with her. My dad is too old to help with him. I'm just losing it." Richie dropped his head.

"I already know the struggle. You got to get home. Send my love out to her to get well."

Richie nodded his head. They gripped hands and hugged. Doing time, the guys around you became your family, but not by blood and you adapted their pain. Richie loaded Phillip down with commissary and he left back to his cell.

Phillip didn't go to chow but fixed himself something to eat and wrote Nova a letter. He explained the latest news and how administration had been taking his earnings out his State pay: 70 percent for child support, 15 percent for gate fee, and even the fees for copies at the law library for his prose motion to the courts, despite his indigence. After the deduction of fees, he would end up with a net income under a dollar and had no room to even buy a bar of soap to wash up.

He wrapped up Nova's letter and got his package together. He gave it to the hallway porter to get it down to him. He enjoyed the solitude of not having a cellmate as he stared at the cream colored wall from his bed. *This is life*, he thought, *just waiting on time*.

He jumped up and acted as if he was dribbling a basketball then shooting it. He was playing in a championship game mentally. Time went by as he entertained himself.

Phillip heard the CO's dangling keys as he passed out the mail on the range. Phillip went to his cell door and looked out the window. He was hoping to receive some words from the outside. When the CO got to his door, Phillip knocked on the door to stop him. The CO stopped with a hand full of mail and stated, "None for you Sanders," and continued on.

Phillip heard laughter from guys who received mail. It reminded him of the joy he felt just from a letter. He searched his brain to see who to write, but he couldn't think of anyone, so he stretched across his mat to rest his mind.

Later on that night, a fly fluttered into his cell. The fly landed on the corner of Phillip's mouth while he was sleep. The fly's tickling feet awake Phillip and he softly smacked his face. The fly zipped through the air and onto his nose. He then realized that it was a fly pestering him. He leaned up and looked for it as he grabbed his shower shoe. He wasn't going back to sleep until he killed it. The disturbance of his sleep had him wrathful and he couldn't chance getting woke back up. There it was—on the toilet seat. He watched it clean his little feet then whacked it and pushed its remains off into the toilet. That killing was as an ice cube to his brain—it cooled him off. He dropped his shower shoe and lay back down.

Phillip woke up bright and early. He didn't go to breakfast this morning because his stomach was satisfied from the meal he ate last night. He thought about going to work, but was turned off when he thought about working for free. Out of the blue, there was a small knock on his door. It was his next door neighbor Cody. Phillip climbed out of the bed, went to the door and opened it.

Cody instantly asked, "What's up? Didn't mean to bother you, but do you have an emery board?"

Phillip hesitated in thought and replied, "Uh, no."

"Okay, I was trying to file these wires down on my headphones."

"Won't you just burn them? Was that you laughing like that last night after mail call?"

"No, that was D-Bo. He had got a letter from an old friend. The letter tickled him to life. But I haven't had any sleep. I've been up three days writing this poem. I want you to check it out. Hold on." He shot into his cell and retrieved the poem. He handed it to Phillip. He read it:

I wake up drenched in sweat
My heart pounding out of my chest
With these nightmares I regret
My mind will never be at rest
The mystery haunts my thoughts
About what happened that tragic night
Revenge is what I want. . .
But who do I owe the fight?
Sometimes I blame myself
As I stare into the mirror
I look for an explanation
But the situation never gets any clearer
I constantly search my conscience
As I desperately try to find a clue
I know I've made some bad decisions
But I never could have hurt you
I've paid the price with my life

And I miss you each and every day
I hear your laughter in my head
And it never fades away
Brandon if you're listening
Know that daddy will never forget you
You own a special place in my heart
And my love for you will always be true.

The end

Phillip had to think for a second what the poem was about. Then it struck him—the meaning of it. Cody was in there for killing his son and everyday it haunted him.

He handed it back and added, "That was very good, very deep. I have something for you to ponder on. What always try to keep itself clean, but stay shitty at the same time?"

Cody tilted his head then glanced at Phillip. "I don't know . . . a person in trouble."

Phillip chuckled. "No. I'm going to let you think more on that. Hey, where's D-Bo at? I need some of that green."

"He's in there." Cody pointed towards his cell.

Phillip stepped over and peeked in the door. He requisition to D-Bo for some marijuana to smoke. D-Bo hooked him up for five dollars in commissary. Phillip was happy, went back to his cell and closed the door. He made some incense out of toilet paper and gel deodorant to burn while he smoked. The THC put him in the mood to write, he had some people he wanted to give a piece of his mind to, but he sat at his desk stuck with the pen in his hand. He eventually went to bed.

Every day at mail time he would stand at the door and watch the CO pass by without stopping and sliding a letter under his door. He was disappointed every time because he psyched himself up that he was receiving mail. He had a thought to act as some of the guys who wrote request slips to the staff just to get mail, but he had nothing to query. *Ain't nobody been writing me, so why the fuck should they start writing me*, he mumbled.

He sat at his desk and wrote his mother a letter of anger: *You say, I didn't tell you to do what you did; you made your bed now lie in it. Well, what did you teach me? You abandon me as a child and expected for me to act as an adult when crime was the only way for me to eat. So are you happy now, that I'm locked up and you think I'm safe and can smoke your dope in peace* . . . At the end he tore it up.

He heard some voices outside his door that escalated into a verbal dispute. He went to the door to see who it was. It was his next door neighbor to the right of him—Westside, and two CO's. Westside was refusing to go back into his cell—he was high off the pills and stressing over his girl cheating. One of the guards tried to shove Westside into his cell. Westside instantly reacted and attacked the officers. He knocked one down with a quick blow and the other guard took off running.

Phillip pressed his face against the small window to see what was going on, but only caught a little action.

Westside went after the officer. He caught him a short distance away and drop kicked him in the back. He was beating the back of the CO's head when the other officers' came and pepper sprayed him then handcuffed him.

Phillip could hear everything that was going on—the guards beating and hauling Westside off. Everyone in their cells was yelling and banging on their doors. It was a moment of great excitement.

The next morning word got back the CO's killed Westside. They had taken him to the hole and continuously spread him with tear gas. The facility's head used their favorite line to the public—he died on the way to the hospital. The prison went on lock down for a few days because of the death. Things of such nature can stir up a deadly riot situation.

Guy's that were friends of Westside was able to call his family and explain what they had known.

Phillip sat at his desk with a pen in hand in thought of the mayhem in America. He began to write: *They can kill us and its okay. Convicted us wrongfully and excuses they only have to say. They just killed another black man today . . . hurray.* The moment Phillip was locked up, his life ended right then. His thoughts were from then and before. He was walking dead. He wrote some more: *Dead and Forgotten. They buried me alive. I hate this place, the walking dead cemetery.*

There was a tap on his door. Phillip's head shot towards it. It was the hallway porter again. He slid a note from Nova under the door and walked away. Nova had thanked Phillip and let him know he received his kite and package.

The letter was right on time, he needed someone to vent to. Immediately he wrote Nova and complained about getting showed no love from the outside world because

how much time he had left he thought. He ended the
missive with:

Crash Course of Life

*What is the point in living when you are in a runaway car
on a dead-end road? It seems your whole life has led up to
the crash course that your life has become. Deep down, you
hope for a malfunction in the car so you won't crash into
that dead-end, but as luck would have it, you're in the best
built car ever. Is there any way to jump out of this speed
demon so you might be able to save yourself? You think,
but the straps seem to tighten around you. And now that
you see the inevitable, the only real decision is to stomp on
the gas and get this fucked up ride they call life over with.
As you pass by the people that once meant something to
you, you hope just once that someone will help you, but this
ride will never slow long enough for you to say goodbye . .
. just wave . . . and they still won 't see you . Maybe you
will see them in the world beyond. Will anyone even miss
you or do they care? Fuck it! If they did care, they would
try to help you stop this runaway car that keeps thundering
down this dead-end road. Yet, their too caught up with
their own ride to care about yours. So just sit back and ride
this ride to the dead-end and beyond. Nobody will ever
notice you're gone until you crash and burn.*

Phillip.

He had the porter take Nova the letter. That night Phillip
had a fearsome dream that shook him out his sleep. He
arose and peered out the rectangular window at outside.
The tall poles were bursting with light at the top of them;

the razor wire fences reflected the gleam making it hard to see anything else but the grass. There wasn't much room anyway to see out—the window was too narrow to get a wide view.

One day I will be out, he thought, as he turned away and got back in the bed. Out of boredom, he masturbated. It helped ease his mind. He was able to get back to sleep after he finished.

The day was boring to Phillip as he sat at his desk and glanced around. He had no TV, no radio, no cards or even a book to read to occupy his mind. It was refreshing anytime he received a letter from Nova because it felt as he was receiving mail.

He had a thought and wrote it out on paper: *Reach for the moon because you can touch it*.

He put down his pen and decided to smoke the last of the weed he had. As he blew out smoke, he sung out loudly, "I want to be freeee. . . ." Everyone on the range heard that and recited it. Phillip smirked and nodded his head. He pulled out some old pictures he had stashed away. Memories of the past flashed through his mind. He began to talk to the pictures as if they were right in front of him. He wanted to know why he was left behind, but he couldn't figure any answer, so he just sent a mental message to ask, *where's the love at*? His heart sung out to the world every night looking for a connection—he wished upon a star.

He knew they would be putting someone in his cell soon and prayed not someone as Stanley, but he couldn't trust anyone no way. He was in there with *real* criminals. Guy's that would go through your property to look for addresses to write, pictures to look at, personal information, and even get comfortable with your mail as they read it, so he couldn't put anything past anyone. *Maybe he will have a TV*, Phillip thought, *but until then, let me try to get my own.*

He wrote out a request slip to the case work manager for a TV loan. He then got himself ready for lunch. When the doors popped, he headed out and dropped the slip inside the mail box by the guard's desk. On the way back from chow, he saw Richie from a distance going the opposite direction. Richie had signaled for Phillip to swing around but the guard instructed to keep moving. Richie yelled, "Mom died today!"

Phillip attempted to walk over to get the scoop, but the CO turned him around. Phillip shouted, "I'll be to holler at you."

About five minutes later after Phillip got back to his block he heard guys talking about Richie just got knocked out. Phillip butted in, in disbelief because he just saw Richie. They added, "He just got knocked out in the chow hall and everybody stood up and counted to ten. Somebody ran right up on Richie and side blinded him."

"What . . . did they lock up the guy who did it?" Phillip asked still bemused.

"No. They didn't catch him. He slid right out the door. The tray cart blocked his way. They didn't take Richie to the hole. They took him over to medical."

Phillip just turned away and walked to his cell. He thought about Richie's mother just dying and this happening to him. He wanted revenge instantly. He knew they would keep Richie down in medical under observation. Phillip began doing push-ups to blow off steam. In between push-ups he wrote Richie a letter to see what actually happen and to let him know he was getting ready for war. He then gave it to the porter to take to him.

Mail time came and Phillip stood at the door to watch the CO go passed him again for the millionth time. He just dropped his head and sat on his bed.

Later on, the porter stopped at his door and knocked. He slid a letter from Richie under his door and left. Phillip read it:

What's up brother? Not much bro. Just sitting down here. I truly don't know what happened. I was hit from behind and knocked out. All I can think of is that they paid someone to jump on me to get me moved so they can have full access to the mule.

I do not owe any $ or nothing. Brother I've been cool and laid back trying to get this $ and this lawyer. I have NO idea who hit me. I have no idea why. I swear that to you brother. I have not done anything wrong.

I love you brother. I am all fucked up over mom dying. I need to be around a phone and now I can't even call for the funeral. Man I am all tore up. Keep your head up. I'll be out there soon.

Phillip couldn't wait for the morning to investigate. He wanted to know who was behind this.

It was morning and he hadn't got that much sleep. His mind was filled with war. He left out the cell bright and early searching for information. He found different version of the story and different people who supposed to had been behind it. He stayed out all day until he had enough information. He wrote Richie back and told him he was about to go at these guys.

He was doing push-ups when he heard a knock on his door. It was the porter with a letter from Nova. Phillip slid Richie's letter under the door and picked up Nova's letter. Phillip unfolded the toilet paper and read it:

Sometimes when you let people down, it's hard for them to get over the pain, so they move on to conceal the grief, and forget about you. So don't bother, for worrying is like a rocking chair, it keeps you busy, but it doesn't get you anywhere. Who cares how much time you have? If someone cares about you, they'll be there. So don't worry about the people who aren't there, be happy about the people who are. It could be worse because the only future I get a glimpse at is these iron bars and gray walls that surround me. But hey, I got you . . . In a world of loneliness Nova.

Phillip reasoned about how Nova could think so positive from the position he was in. He soothed Phillip's mind as he thought about his life. *A few more years and this is over with*, Phillip concluded.

He went back to plotting on how to get the guy who done this to Richie. If he had the chance to get a hold to the right one, he would kill him. It was a mentality prison put in your head—to be murderous.

He opened his cell door to take a short stroll on the range one last time before they had to lock it down for the night. There was Cody standing there as soon as he stepped foot out. Cody saw something on Phillip's mind and asked,

"Hey what's up? What's wrong?"

Phillip kept a straight face and answered, "What's up. Nothing," then swayed his head.

Suddenly, Freaky T walked up and hugged Cody from the back. Shocked, Phillip drew his head back. *What the fuck*, Phillip thought. *If he tries to hug me like that, I'm going to turn a flip.*

"What's up?" Freaky T greeted. He let the long paused hug go from Cody and nodded at Phillip. Cody slowly turned around. Freaky T said to Cody, "Come holler at me in a minute before lock down," and then walked off to his cell.

Phillip asked, "You be dealing with dude like that?"

"I talk to him here and there. He be hooking me up with different things."

"You know he wants something in return? What do you be getting from him anyways?"

"Freaky T's cool. He be looking out for me whenever I'm hungry, let me listen to his walkman, and throwing me new shirts and draws anytime they look dingy."

Cody was as a booty bandit like them—white, cute, frail, with a plump backside. Phillip stared at Cody in suspicion of Freaky T getting a hold of him. Phillip inquired, "So, how did he come at you?"

Cody thought Phillip knew he became Freaky T's secret lover by his question, but he knew if D-Bo found out, he would kick him out the cell. He hesitated in thought of how he was going to gather his words and spoke shyly, "One day I got a note slid under my door. This was before D-Bo was my Celly. Freaky T was standing at the door as he pointed down at the note and walked away. I opened the note and read it. It said, 'I'm about to go to the shower in five minutes, pull down your pants, lay across your bed so I can see your ass—'"

Abruptly, two inmates came running down the range. Cody and Phillip pressed their backs against the wall. The Aztec native had a knife in his hand chasing the guy who stole something out his cell.

Phillip and Cody both watched them fly down the range until they were out of sight. Cody said astonished, "Wow, are they serious?" He giggled and put his hand over his mouth. "I was on the basketball court today—"

"Hold on, wait a minute. What did you do about the note?" Phillip cut him off to get back to the topic. *I know he whooped dudes ass*, he thought.

Cody looked at Phillip and said, "I pulled my pants down and let him see my ass."

Phillip was instantly disgusted. "What!" Phillip frowned at him with one eye brow raised.

"He just wanted to see my ass. I had to, I was hungry."

"Fuck that. I just knew you was going to say you beat'em up."

"You heard about what happen with the coffee right?"

"No. What about it?"

"You heard the story about in the chapel for the bag of coffee," Cody expressed as if he was sure he heard about it.

"No. I didn't. What happen?"

"Man, Billy's shit about this big." He used his fingers to indicate a small size penis. "I want do it again."

"What?"

"I sucked Billy's dick for a bag of coffee."

"For a bag of coffee," he uttered in a low tone and

shook his head. "Man get the fuck away from me." Phillip wanted to punch Cody but saved the hostile energy for another battle. He turned and stepped into his cell as he slammed the door. The door rattled the whole range. He was fired up. "What the fuck he telling me that shit for, is he hitting on me or wanting to suck my dick?" Phillip grumbled.

He flopped on his bed and stared at the wall. He was tired of being in bondage. His mind was being eating away by bitterness. It was a dying feeling—very painful. There wasn't anything for him to do but watch his life go by.

About an hour after locked down, the CO came walking down the range with the mail. *Today is the day and I better have some mail*, Phillip thought. He stood at the door to watch the guard walk by—and that's what he did—walked by. At that moment, he was dying mentally. He was crushed by what he already knew—that he wasn't going to receive any mail—but his wishful thinking lifted him up so he could come crashing down. He stepped back and shouted, "Fuck the world!" His voice echoed down the range. He took off his shirt and threw it against the wall. He jerked his arm forward then plopped on his bed and rock back and forth. *If I just kill myself I wouldn't have anything to worry about*, he contemplated.

It was lunch time and Phillip rested under his covers. He planned to stay under them all day because he didn't want to face the world. A few of his friends came pass to see if he was going to lunch, but he just waved them off. He was just going to eat one of the few Ramon Noodle Soups he had left in peace.

Out of the blue, a paper slid under his door and then

there was a loud knock on his door. Phillip moved the covers from his head and peered at the door. It was the porter pointing down at the letter on the floor and then took off. Phillip got up and picked up the letter. It was from Richie.

Hey Bro, is this their definition of a hit!? Are you serious? A cracked nasal cavity and black eye. Uh-oh, now they got the liger and the lion plotting some sick shit.

Brother I'm so lost and truly destroyed behind mom's death. I have to get out. I cannot continue to play these gay politics. How can I function on the level of those around us. Just as I think I'm out they Pull me back in. AHHH! Have these sheep actually rocked themselves to sleep thinking it is okay to slap a lion and then go to sleep with him. I am growling inside and it is taking all of my energy and concentration to stay focused. I want to take it down a stupid fucked up road, but my intelligence knows the outcome and I must base my decision on knowledge and not on being reactionary. Using my head in this way is different and is very difficult.

Phillip, I'm trembling inside wanting revenge. I want to do some sick shit that will make any other demonstrations of the past pale in comparison. However, it will go down in history and only add to the legends they tell about us already and keep us in prison even longer.

Now here you are! P! My one true FRIEND. I can feel the love you have for me. I can see you working out and plotting mad hood violence on those who hurt me. That gives me strength and I will always uphold our friendship and keep the bond between us . . . simply unbreakable. I usually resort to a "Survival of self" mode in life altering situations. Yet here I find myself including your life and how my decision will affect you directly. Phillip, I love you and want to see you free. Your spirit is identical to mine and I cannot be responsible for (1) single minute of your incarceration. I understand that some situations are just unavoidable. Others are more difficult where pride is concerned, but I am a Master of ME, and I know what resides within me and I do not have to expose it unless I feel it is a must. Not to prove it exists to other people. These clowns want me to explode so they can have a story to tell and don't give a fuck about my kids, your freedom or anything pertaining to anything other than their entertainment. I have to get home, you have to get out. There are a lot of roads to choose from in this situation. However, I will not choose one that fucks us over. So just leave it up to me. See you soon. Love your Brother Richie

The letter eased his mind but he was still edgy and ready to get the guy who put this together. He lay back down and went to sleep.

Two weeks past and Phillip spent most of the time in his cell. He was sitting at his desk beating on it as he rhymed when the CO came to the door. The guard opened it and handed him a pass to go see the case work manager. Phillip didn't know what it was for and got ready then headed out.

To his surprise, the case work manager gave Phillip a TV loan. The pacifier brought joy to Phillip. He thanked him and scampered on his way as he carried the TV.

When he got back to his cell door, he opened D-Bo's

cell to let him know the news, but found Cody lying on the floor against the toilet bleeding from his arms.

He rushed into Cody's cell and put the TV on the desk. Phillip grabbed Cody's towel and T-shirt off his bed. He began to apply pressure on the open flesh wombs were Cody cut himself.

Cody opened his eyes and whispered, "I want to be freeee. Let me be freeee."

"No, it's going to be okay. You're going to make it." He turned his head towards the door and yelled, "Help! Help! Somebody get the CO!"

Cody peering at Phillip lackadaisical mumbled, "You never told me what keeps its self-clean, but stay shitty at the same time."

As Phillip tied the shirt around Cody's arm, he replied, "A fly . . . it's a fly."

"Oh." Cody chuckled.

A few prisoners heard Phillip's cry and came running. When they looked in the cell, one of them took off to tell the officer while the other one came in and helped. A short time later, the cell was swarmed with CO's and nurses. Phillip went back into his cell with his TV and shut his door. After Cody was taken away, he was allowed to take a shower.

Phillip dragged his feet back to his cell in his shower shoes and boxer shorts; his towel was laid across his shoulder. He flung his door closed. He finished drying his top half off then plugged his TV up. He flicked through the stations until he found something he thought was interesting. He sat on his bunk and dried his feet as he watched TV.

Later on that night he didn't get up to watch the CO pass with the mail. He was lost in the visional drama the TV showed. When 11:00 p.m. came around, he turned to the news. A breaking news alert displayed. It had been a murder and they were on the scene. Unexpectedly, the news caster named Phillip's friend as the murdered victim. When he heard that, he jumped up and glued his eyes to the TV. His friend's name echoed through his mind. Phillip was positive it was him when he saw his friend's family. He dropped his head and put his arms on his knees.

Five days later. It was mail time and Phillip stood at the door waiting on the CO to pass, but today, the guard stopped at his door and dropped a letter on the floor and kicked it under his door. Phillip looked at the guard as if this couldn't be true, then picked it up. It had been stamped showing that a money order was taken out in the amount of 100 dollars. Phillip looked at the name—it was his friend that just passed five days ago. He quickly opened the letter and read it. He had informed Phillip on what was going on in the streets and what he was doing.

Phillip took it as his last words before his death. This letter he will always keep and value. The only person on the outside that showed love died right after he showed it. He read the letter over and over as he shed tears. Phillip felt as he lost himself. He lay down to rest the pain away.

At the top of the morning, the officer unlocked and opened Phillip's cell door. Phillip heard someone dragging their personal belongings. Today was the day he got a cellmate. The guard stated as he pushed the door wide opened, "Here you go."

Phillip pulled the covers from his head and peered at the doorway. It was Stanley standing there with all his property

COURAGE
AND
DETERMINATION

We as people have to understand we have our ups and downs, and we cannot kick each other when we see one down, but help lift that person up. So it's understandable when you see someone down to help them up, especially when that person is trying to help themselves up. Ambition—potential of a star that person has trying to fight through the struggle to make it to the top. The hard work he or she has to put in, the slips, the falls, the strength used to get back up, and the punishing efforts to the finish line. Does that person always come in first? No, but he or she finishes. So to the people who don't have to go through a struggle need to take heed to the people who do, and go after your goals. For there is no reason to wait, but act. A reminder—pleasure will come later.

Just some thoughts I had, next . . .

VIOLATION

There are some things in life
you just have to choose from.

Carol better known to the boys as Candy, stood in front
of the stainless steel sink adding black eyeliner to his
arched eye brows. He sung in a whisper the song "Thinking
about you" by Frank Ocean that played over his clear boom
box radio sitting on top of his desk as he leaned close to the
mirror.

"Yes of course, I remember, how could I forget how
you feel. You know you were my first time, a new feel...."

A pair of special made thongs hung from a clothes line
in front of the small window and the morning sun shone in
his well-kept cell. His bed was made tightly—you could
bounce a quarter on his white thermo blanket and colorful
throw rugs laid across the floor giving the cell warmth.

Candy smoothed on lip gloss, puckered his lips, touched
his hair that was in a bun, and then lustfully swayed his
head as if he was the most gorgeous thing in the world. He
smacked his backside giddily. The gray jogging pants he
wore were skinny fit, including his white tee shirt. He was
trying to be something he hated—a female.

He tidied up everything before he left out his cell. He
had just entered onto the range putting two starburst into
his month when he heard the altercation going on in a cell

down the range. He perceived his friend—Buttons—shrill cry for someone to stop. He immediately trotted to Buttons cell.

BOOM!

Buttons' cell door exploded open. Candy jumped back quickly to get out the way.

Rick came bouncing off the door then charging back into the room. Buttons stood in between two lovers to stop them from fighting.

Candy galloped into the cell to assist and pulled Rick back by his shoulders. Buttons was relieved to see Candy and pushed Ted onto the bed to put an end to this.

"Rick, won't you stop! Just gooo!" Buttons pleaded throwing his hand out praying to God he would just leave.

"I see how you want to play. It's over," Rick said with a frown, and pulled away from Candy then padded down the range.

Ted stood and grasped Buttons by the shoulders. Buttons pushed Ted's arms away and said, "That wasn't called for—"

"I thought I was the only one—"

"Ted, I just want to be by myself right now. I'll talk with you later. Bye." Buttons looked at Ted and waved dismissing him. Ted gave a look of disapproval and then stepped out glaring at Candy as if he was the cause of this.

Candy sauntered over to Buttons and asked, "Girl, you all right?"

Buttons stumbled back and fell onto his bed. "I can't believe this shit just happen to me. I was kicking it with Ted and Rick just came through out of nowhere."

"I heard you scream. I didn't know what was going on.

But that's what happens when you want to be a playa. You got to be ready to handle the heat honey."

"It ain't that. It just something about them two I can't leave alone." Buttons began to weep.

Candy reached over and grabbed a roll of toilet paper. He handed it to Buttons and expressed, "You're gonna have to choose. You got two thugs that ain't going to back down. Which one do you like the most?"

Buttons stood up in his tightly fitted gray jogging pants and white tee shirt wiping his eyes. He returned, "I don't know. When Ted first pushed in my button . . . bitch . . . I fell in love. And Rick, he just talked me right out my panties with his fine ass."

"Mmm . . . You dick whipped with some serious issues. Well, we got to meet up with Detroit on the yard and give him that package, then meet up with the girls at the gym. Get yourself together so we can dip. I'm about to go grab the stuff." Candy lithe switched out the cell as he stuck out his chest as if he had breast. He retrieved the package and then they headed out to the yard.

Candy and Buttons met up with Detroit and delivered him the last of his package. They held the drugs for different penitentiary hustlers and made good money doing so.

They shifted to the gym to meet the other girlish men of the institution. Candy playfully danced up to their two friends Sue and Skittles.

Sue shouted, "Oh shit bitch! Go head!" They all giggled.

Buttons greeted, "What's up with you bitches?"

Skittles, their Caucasian friend out the bunch, dressed in small white shorts that showed his thighs, and a halter top, campily replied with a question, "Where you two bitches coming from dressed like twins?"

Candy informed, "From the cell blocks, yard." He noticed the blonde streaks in Sue's hair and ambled over to him in amusement. "Girl, where did you get this from?"

"From my man," Sue said as he put his hand on his hip. His white boyfriend had cut his hair off and gave it to him.

Buttons spoke, "Robby cut his hair off for you?"

"Yes, my baby went bald for me. I had to put the blonde streaks in my hair. Since he did that, I got his name tattooed on my chest." Sue pulled his tee shirt down to confirm the tattoo.

Skittles remarked, "That's what happens when they taste the rainbow. Sue and Robby's in love and we're going to hold the wedding for them." He smiled.

"Then me and my Boo is going on a honeymoon."

Candy happy for Sue couldn't hold back the news about Buttons, he induced, "Fabulous, but ya'll need to help your sister Buttons on some game because she was all into it this morning and had me in the middle of it."

"What? In the middle of what? What's going on?" Skittles questioned as his eyes shot over at Buttons.

Buttons put his hand on his hip then snapped his fingers with his free hand at Candy and said, "Un uh, it ain't nothing. She just mad 'cause she can't get no man—"

"No man! I get holler all day long. I just don't settle for anything like someone else," Candy snapped back.

"No she didn't. The situation earlier wasn't anything major. Me and Ted was chilling and Rick came through. It turned into a fight between the two. She help break it up and Rick just a slap dick," Buttons explained.

Sue uttered, "You got two of them fighting over you, you go girl. Yeah, if Rick's a slap dick then you're slap dick-ted." They all laughed except for Buttons.

Buttons ready to go asked, "Come on, let's get to business. What's the plan?"

Skittles replied, "Well, they supposed to be shaking down the cell blocks today or tomorrow, so we got these packs to hold and four phones. I got everything wrapped and ready. Let's go to the restroom. You hoes got to douche first."

"My pussy clean," Candy stated, as they amusingly strutted to the restroom.

Sue handed Candy and Buttons Hot Sauce bottles and said, "You know what to do. Make sure it's clean."

They had to use the Hot Sauce bottles to clean their rectum. They filled the bottles up with water out the sink then sat on the toilets next to each other. The toilets were divided by a four foot wall.

Two known gang members walked in the restroom and glanced at Candy and Buttons squeezing water up their booties and grimaced. "What the fuck," Joker muttered.

Candy being goofy put the Hot Sauce bottle on top of the divider and asked, "Can one of ya'll fill this up?" then pointed at the sink with the bottle. "With water."

"What!" Joker exclaimed and laughed. "I'm not putting my hands on that." His friend Guda looked on with a grin.

Buttons shouted, "Fill mines up too!"

Joker replied, "Ya'll trippin'. Keep up the good work." Joker and Guda went to the urinals and stared up at the ceiling as they urinated. Joker being a wisecracker glanced over at Candy and said, "Is that a French bun on top of your head?" then snickered. "I heard they call you super head around this muthafucka. You don't got no fire head."

"Honey please, I have all types of request slips in this muthafucka. Its ninety degrees right now, it's too hot to be gay."

Joker and Guda both laughed as they finished up.

Candy kept his eyes on Guda as he got off the toilet. He ogled at Guda as he sauntered up on the two. Candy pulled the empty bottle from behind his back and said, "It eliminates all odors. Did ya'll eat that chicken yesterday?"

They both simultaneously said, "Yeah."

"Well, it's just like the chicken. It slides right off the balls." Candy bent over and acted as if he squeezed the bottle in his ass.

"Oh hell naw, we got to get the fuck up out of here," Joker said and started out the restroom. Guda struck off behind him, but turned and gave Candy a wink on the way out the door.

Candy went crazy inside and grasped his chest. "Buttons, you see that?"

"What?" Buttons asked as he got up off the John pulling his jogging pants up.

"That fine man just winked at me."

"Who? The short one that was talking shit?"

"Noooo, the tall one."

"Girl please, ain't nobody winking at you. Let's pack this stuff and move on." They both put a thick wrapped package and a phone up their cavity then headed back to their cells.

Early the next morning, the Emergency Squad—better known as the E-Squad—dressed in black swat gear trudged down the range. They pulled each prisoner out their cell one by one. Each inmate had to get naked and that was right up Candy's ally.

Candy unclothed, came out the cell with his hands on top of his head as he made his butt bounce in rhythm to disgust the guards.

The whole swat team turned their heads and instructed Candy to put on his boxer shorts. They did a quick search and got Candy back into his cell.

Candy smiled picking his things up off the floor as he knew his gayness always worked, but his mind reverted to Guda. He was eager to go back out to see if he saw him again. *He's tall, built, sexy, and mixed*, Candy thought. *I can get the best of both races*. He wanted Guda to be his lover to shut Buttons up, and it was a challenge he was up for. He ship-shaped his cell then relaxed back to watch TV.

Days went past before lock down was over from the institutional shake down. When the cell doors popped, Candy and Buttons met up to head down to meet up with Sue and Skittles.

They gave the packages up and got their money in return. Candy was anxious to go into the gym to see if he saw Guda, but he wasn't there, just a bunch of guys playing basketball and working out. They decided to go back to their cells because Buttons had a pass to go to medical.

When Candy made it back to his cell door, he saw Guda coming down his range with a laundry bag in hand.

He must be picking up a debt, Candy thought.

Candy stared at Guda as he strolled pass him with a mysteries grin on his face. "Hi," Candy said, but was late with his words. Guda kept walking but glanced back at Candy before he was out of sight.

This was the first time Candy ever acted shy and felt as if he just stabbed himself in the heart. He stepped into his cell and shut the door. When he took his next step, he heard crumbling paper at his feet. He looked down and found a note on the floor. He picked it up and read it:

Look I'm 45 yrs old. Been locked up since I was 18. Only been with two (2) woman & never even thought about fucking a boy until I saw you. I'd talk to you all the time if I didn't have this prison rep to stand up to. Stay in bed until everyone leaves at breakfast. The ranges will empty out then just look for me & we'll go there. I want to stand behind you, lick your ass a few times then fuck. It'll be quick so I'll try to fuck twice. I got some cocaine I can give you and some food for missing chow. I need to fuck you. Hope to see you not go. Just a lil fellow, it won't hurt you. Couldn't hand this to you. 2morrow breakfast!! Let me know if you want the cocaine 2day.

Who put this right here, Candy wondered. He plumped his bottom onto his bed. *It's somebody trying to be funny*, he reckoned, *but was it him—Guda*? He read the letter one last time before he added his money up by the drugs he received in payment.

The next morning Candy stayed in for breakfast, but the secret admire didn't show. Candy had prepared for him—the cell window was draped in royal blue curtains—a stick incent burned over the sink—and his radio played sweet melodies.

Candy peeked out his door in his small white tee shirt and pink panties. The range was bright and empty. He became down casted because he thought he had action, but he knew if he wanted action, he had to go find it. Plus, he wanted to show Buttons he gets holler as well. He planned to leave out this morning and stay out until he bumped into Guda.

The blinding sun was rising in the clear blue sky. The yard was partially filled with men running around the track, shooting ball, exercising on the pull up bars, and standing around socializing.

Candy dressed in skin tight state pants, a v-neck tee shirt, and white low cut shoes, strolled the yard looking for Guda as he kicked little rocks.

Guda wasn't anywhere to be found and Candy got tired in his search for him. He sat on the bleachers inside the track area and peered up at the sky at the airplanes soaring passed. *Only if I could enjoy this moment with Guda*, Candy thought.

Surprisingly, Guda trotted onto the track. Candy's eyes went wide. *There he goes*, Candy thought, as he wiggled in his seat.

Guda in his gray gym shorts and running sneakers threw his wife beater into the grass and began jogging around the track.

Candy peered at Guda's tattoos on his body as he jogged. He waited until Guda ran a few laps before he stepped out the bleachers and onto the track.

Candy caught Guda by surprise as he jogged up behind Candy and slowed into a walking pace.

Candy acted startle and said, "Oh my God! You scared me."

Guda stepped to the side and replied, "My bad." He looked deeply at Candy's high cheek bones, his features were as a woman's, and his demeanor made him the next best thing to a woman.

Candy blushed and campily said, "I wasn't paying any attention." He gazed at Guda's body and the light sheen of sweat that covered it. "They say sweat does a body good. Are you enjoying your work out?"

Guda was being penalized by his gang and had to complete whatever workout they demanded. He returned, "Not really, I owe twenty laps for talking bad to one of my brothers. So I'm trying to knock this out so I can go on about my day."

Any conversation the girlish men of the institution got, they took it as someone was trying to holler at them. *Did he drop that note in my cell*, Candy thought. So he pressed, "Can I work out with you?"

"No thanks." He frowned at Candy.

Candy took off running as he poked out his booty to entice Guda. Candy stopped and said, "Come on, I can run too."

Guda laughed and expressed, "I'm cool," then began to pick up his pace.

Candy ogled at him as Guda caught up and suggested,

"If you ever need somebody to hold anything for you, just let me know. I got you."

"All right." Guda took back off running.

Candy stood there in a daze as he watched Guda run around the track. *Damn, what the fuck!* Candy thought. *What about the winks?* Then he figured, *Guda didn't want anyone to see him hollering at me because of his gang.* He knew Guda's gang was connected with moving a lot of drugs through the prison and they would need some holders. He sauntered off in thought of seeing Guda again.

Buttons, Skittles, and Candy strolled down the range chitchatting about relationships and the prison gay life.

The thing about prison gays was they didn't try to find a husband but someone to mesh around with for a couple hours, just really look for a fling because all the ones who wanted relationships were considered psychopaths, and the clandestine thugs were considered creatures—creatures of the night. They never let their gayness come too light— whatever they did needed to be done in the dark.

" . . . You sexed enough first timers to know by now," Buttons ventilated to Candy.

"Yeah, yeah, I'm going to get my king, I'm just waiting to catch him again and wrestle him down," Candy said in return to Buttons *hating* on him.

"Girl, you don't know what to say to him that's why you can't get'em," Buttons induced. "You have to come up with some lines that leave him in wonder. I once told a guy after seeing him in the shower, I wanted him to use his dick like a baseball bat and beat my ass hole up like it was a Piñata."

They came upon a flight of stairs and easily stepped down them.

With his brashly attitude Skittles added, "Yesss, you have to set the tone because those first timers be scared shitless. But once I break'em, anyone can ride'em."

"I haven't had the right opportunity," Candy contended.

"They be acting brand new around their homeboys, but when you get that chance to get one on one, you have to seize the moment," Buttons coached. "When I first done Ted's hair, he told me his girl had left him and he knew he still could pull'em anyway. I leaned down and whispered in his ear, you're not lying. Mmm." He moved his head like a rollercoaster.

"You ain't the only one that can get'em," Skittles uttered. "All the boys love me. Once one burns out, you just screw in another one. I tell'em like this, even if they need a warm place to piss in the winter time, they can stick it in me."

They came upon the dayroom area and there was a group of men standing there talking. It was one dude Skittles been chasing for a long time in the crowd—Nati.

"Ooh, there goes Nati," Skittles whispered as he pointed at the crowd of men. "I want him soo bad, I can taste him. Go over there and talk to them. I'm gonna pull the medical trick."

Candy switched over to the crowd as Buttons and Skittles designed the game plan.

"Gentlemen, at the end of the rainbow is a pot of gold," Candy phrased in the most feminine mannerism.

Three dudes grimaced and simultaneously spoke, "Yeah, a pot of doo doo."

"You look like Lebron James."

"Who called him over here?"

"Uh, excuse me," Candy said before anyone could speak again. "You better get your pronouns right talking about him. You mean she." He twisted his facial features.

"You looking too strong to be a she—" one of the guys's said then was cut off by his friend.

"Ol' basketball playing mu'fucka." All of them busted out laughing.

Candy came back, "Anyone for a game of one on one—"

"Girl! Are you all right," Buttons asked Skittles as he grasped his forehead and stumbled around. Buttons walked next to Skittles with his arms out to pretend to catch him if he were to fall.

Everyone looked on.

Skittles stumbled and fainted right into Nati's arms and body.

"What the fuck," Nati muttered as he looked down at Skittles face pressed against his chest. He pushed Skittles up and out his arms then smacked him to the floor. All the gayness eluded Skittles mind.

Buttons and Candy was in awe and ambled over to help skittles.

"Oh girl, you okay?" Buttons said with his hand on Skittles' shoulder.

"I know he care about me now. Every man that loved me, beat me," Skittles said as he held his bruised face.

The guys all moved away and went about their business, most of them laughing.

Candy and Buttons helped Skittles up and to his cell. It

was count time so they both had to go to their cells.

Candy danced around in his cell listening to "Da Butt"
by EU, as he looked at himself in the acrylic mirror that
was in his hand. "Ain't nothing wrong with doing in da
butt all night long . . ." Candy sung as he pushed out his
butt.

Count time had passed and there was a knock on his
door. Candy froze and glanced at his door window, but
didn't see anyone. He shuffled to his door at the same time
another knock sounded and then Guda's head popped in
and pronounced, "Knock. Knock. Can I come in?"

Candy lit up like a Christmas tree as he sighed, lost his
breath and put his hand over his chest. "Yes . . . uh, come
right in." He was caught by surprise. Candy wouldn't have
thought in a billion years this would have played out this
way. He couldn't have asked for any better way. "Hold on
let me turn this down." He took a couple of steps and
squatted to turn off the radio. His skinny fit shirt lifted up
and his shorts lowered showing the crack of his butt.

As Guda watched, he saw the tattoo on Candy's lower
back and ass and asked, "What's that tattoo of on your
back?"

Candy bounced up and replied, "It's a pair of boxing
gloves that goes from my lower back onto my ass, wit,
BEAT IT UP over it. See, look." He turned, pulled his shirt
up and shorts down halfway.

Guda stared more at the crack of Candy's ass than the
tattoo. Guda said, "Boxing gloves," and giggled. "Beat it
up."

Candy pulled up his shorts and asked, "Okay . . . what

brings you?"

Guda pulled up the door and said, "You said if I needed something held to holler at you." He put his hand under his shirt and into his pants. He pulled out a small package wrapped in plastic. "Is this too much for you to hold?"

Candy ogled at him and thought, *this is my time to shine*. "That's not big enough. I got that covered."

"What will it take to fill you up?"

"A solid nine."

"I got that and more."

"Well, we will have to work something out."

"I will come back tomorrow to pick it up. Let me get up out of here, I got some business to handle."

Handle this business here, Candy thought. "Okay, I got you. I'll put it right inside me."

When Guda left out his cell, Candy fell back onto his bed in disbelief that Guda was just in his room.

Early next morning Guda came by Candy cell to pick up the package. He watched Candy squat and pop the package out his derriere. He noticed the package was clean.

Candy took the package out the plastic it was in and handed it to Guda.

Guda smelt it and didn't smell any odor. *Impressive*, Guda thought.

It was time for the moment of truth, the punch line to his destiny, to finally shut Buttons up.

"How long have you been down?" Candy asked standing in front of Guda.

"Three years."

"That's a long time to be down without a blow job. Did

you ever imagine you would go that long?"

"I never thought about it." The thought of having his Johnson sucked jumped in his mind.

"See my sex life doesn't have to stop when I get locked up," Candy said as he sauntered over and put some toilet paper over his cell door window. "I have talents like a magician. I can make things disappear, plus, I don't kiss and tell. Your secret would be safe with me, let me show you."

Guda didn't reject when Candy started fumbling around with his pants. Before he knew it, he was hard and in Candy's mouth. He went against everything he believed in. It felt so wrong but so right.

Candy had reached his goal and enjoyed the taste of his captured creature.

Guda was ashamed and pleasured, after the excitement, speechless and confused. There wasn't much said before he left.

Candy lounged across his bed with Guda's flavor on his tongue and thoughts of what just happen until he dozed off.

Candy had been resting in his cell a few days and stayed to himself. Buttons noticed the length of sleep Candy had been getting and barged into Candy's cell to see what was up.

"Bitch get up, you always sleeping," Buttons said as he shook Candy out his sleep.

"Bitch, I'm pregnant," Candy said coming into consciousness. "What's going on?"

"What's going on with you? You acting like you had some or something."

"I have."

"Ooh . . . from who?"

"I told you I was going to get my king."

"Shut up. Un uh, you for real?"

"Yep."

"Un uh, you got to get up and tell me about this." He sat on the desk stool.

Candy got up and told Buttons about his time with Guda. Buttons was excited for Candy but questioned where he was going to go from here with him. Candy hadn't thought about it but was ready to leave out the cell so he could see Guda. He hadn't seen him in a few days. Candy got himself together and headed out with Buttons.

Guda was shooting pool in the rec hall by himself when Candy located him. Candy approached Guda softly and seductively. "Hi," Candy whispered. Buttons stood back at a distance with a grin on his face.

"What's up?"

"Been thinking about you."

"Same here, just out here waiting on somebody to bring me this money." He looked around to see if anyone was watching. "What brings you out?"

"I wanted to know if you needed me to hold anything?"

"Uh, come back in about thirty minutes, I will have something for you."

"Okay." Candy walked out the rec hall with Buttons. They never noticed Guda's gang members watching the whole merrymaking.

Candy and Buttons went out and burned thirty minutes away by walking around the track talking. They came back to the rec hall and picked up the package from Guda.

Buttons now sure Candy wasn't lying about messing around with Guda.

The next day Guda came to Candy's cell to pick up the package. Instantly, Candy pushed Guda against the wall and began kissing him.

"I want to put that big dick in my mouth," Candy softly smoothed out, as he gripped Guda's penis through his pants.

He started to ease down when somebody yelled out, "Emergency count!"

"Damn," Candy sputtered out.

"I have to go."

Guda got the package and crept out the cell, but was seen from a distance by one of his gang members. Candy peeked out the cell door at Guda until he was out of sight.

After count Joker and a few more gang members charged into Guda's cell. Joker strongly questioned Guda about being in the punk's cell. Guda explained he was holding different packages for them and that was it. Before Joker and the rest of the gang left, Joker made a threat that if he found out any different, Guda was going to get violated in the worst way—close to death.

Guda in fear for his rep and life sent a message to Candy to meet him at the gym.

Guda paced back and forth in the gym as he waited for Candy. When he saw Candy enter the gym, he made eye contact and went inside the restroom.

"What's going on?" Candy asked when he sauntered into the restroom looking at Guda.

Guda acting nervous replied, "You got to fall back. I will pull up on you."

"Fall back. What are you talking about?"

"I'm going to get violated if I be seen wit you again."

"So this is what it's all about, scared of what others think about you. I don't care what they think about me because I'm living for me."

"That's cool and all for you, but it's just too much for me."

"That's how it always is in the beginning, you gonna hear it all then it dies down."

"They're going to kill me if I get violated. It's over. It's over," Guda said throwing his hands out.

Candy's voice got louder as he said, "It's over, shitting me it's over."

"Look, it was cool but this the end—"

"I'm going to set your ass out, tell all your buddies—"

Guda's anger went through the roof. He swung a wild punch barely connecting to Candy's face. Candy unfazed began to throw wild blows back. It looked as a cat fight with their windmill style and missed swings.

An inmate heard the altercation and came inside the restroom and broke it up. He damn near got in a fight with them because they wouldn't stop. The word spread quick, that Guda and the punk was fighting in the gym's restroom.

Guda could hear the footsteps of the men in his gang as they approached his cell door. They ordered him to put his shoes on and escorted him outside to the track where everyone in his gang awaited him.

Guda was grilled about the fight he had with Candy. He

told them the punk lost some of his package in return. But they didn't believe him, so they sent someone to go get Candy.

They all stood in front of the bleachers, Guda, his gang, and Candy.

"What's going on between ya'll two?" Joker asked.

"I have him hold the packs. Somehow some of the product came up short. He wanted to talk crazy and I wasn't going for it," Guda said in desperation to save his life hoping Candy didn't do what he said he was going to do—set him out.

Candy just stood there with his arms folded and leg moving uncontrollably, his facial expression was aggravated.

"You got something to say about this?" Joker asked Candy.

Candy didn't say a word and it was equal to setting him out.

Everyone in the gang could tell they had something going on. The leader stepped up and said, "We're going to give you a fair shake. You got to choose. We know you dealing with the punk. We ain't mad at you." He was using reverse psychology to get the truth out. "So what's it going to be . . . us . . . or the guy with the beard and the bun?"

Guda felt guilty and knew he couldn't go back if he did choose the gang, but there was a strong possibility. He looked over at Candy then glanced over at his awaiting gang. This was like choosing between life and death.

"Candy," Guda mumbled and took a big gulp. Gaining his confidence for acceptance he uttered, "I'm going to roll with candy," and then put his head down.

"All right, meet us in the gym to take your violation." The gang stormed off to the gym.

Candy smiled at Guda as he walked away.

Before they violated him, they told Guda to fight back. He did but it was too many of them. They punched, kicked, and stumped Guda unconsciously and left him on the floor for the CO's to pick up.

After Guda got out of medical all bandaged up, he pro-ceeded to Candy's cell.

Candy had just came out his cell when he noticed Guda limping down his range.

Guda approached Candy with a spiritless limp and puppy dog expression. He was expecting a hug and soft kiss for his wounds.

"I'm here," Guda expressed in a low tone.

Candy still hurt from Guda telling him that it was over wanted to play mind games with Guda to give him a taste of his own medicine. "It's over," Candy said and pushed his fingers out to shoo Guda away.

"What? It's over. Look at me, I almost died."

"You wanted me to fall back remember."

"But I chose you." He cringed almost falling to his knees from his injuries.

"You don't tell me when it's over. I tell you when it's over. When your ass got violated, that's when your ass was booted off the island. Anyways, you was just the flavor of the week."

"You was my first time, a new feel."

"Like Taylor Swift said, 'we are never ever getting back together.'"

Guda heart broke smacked Candy to the floor. He jumped on top of Candy and began choking him. He snarled, "I took a violation for you."

ENVY

If I'm so guilty
Why do they have to lie to the public to convict me
Why do they have to plant evidence
To deceive thee
I'm talking detectives to the police chief
Fabricating every little story about me
Just to incarcerate me and throw away the key
Is it envy
Because all I see is black people around me
You have your few shades of whites
And different colors of light brown
But its majority black people that make up this town
I'm talking prison cells to dormitories
Don't forget about the young ones in the reformatories
The black women too
Just take a second and examined it with a bird's eye view
So is the justice system acts really true
Because most crimes are committed by
Who
Say that then my shirt reads
Please preach to the young
So they won't have to go to the pin
Because the laws are designed to lock up blacks
Over and over again
Slavery is prohibited
except for those whose been convicted
And this just some spoken words my friend
Because we all been hit with some harsh sentences

JUSTICE

Freedom is everything.

Kicks, punches, and elbows thrashed from every direction upon the helpless man balled up on his cell room floor. Dontay and his running buddies—Rico and Chris, battered the man until they thought the message was clear—have Dontay's money on time.

Dontay kicked the man one last time in the back and said in an angry voice, "You must thought it was a game, next time have my shit. And it's double." He stepped broadly out the man's cell along with Rico and Chris.

Dontay took baby steps as he brushed his white tee shirt and khaki pants with his hand and pulled his pants below his rear. The three young men was excited but tried to mask it. They gripped hands and scampered to Dontay's cell.

When they reached the cell, Dontay swung the door opened and headed straight for the boom box sitting on the floor. He turned it on and turned the volume up. Rico sat on the toilet as Chris pulled the door closed and sat on the bed.

Dontay short with a muscular physique and cocky, grooved around as if he was performing on stage in front of Chris as they all recited the rap song "Crazy World" by Young Jeezy, that screamed out the boom box speakers.

"Damn I'm in a trap and these busters trying to punish

us, send a little message out to each and every one of us, real G shit, what I speak is unheard of, when you get more time for selling dope than murder, in this crazy world . . ."

Dontay jerked his arm forward as if he just threw a baseball and shouted, "In this crazy world!" He was lost in the music.

Chris waved his hand at Dontay and pointed at the boom box. Dontay stopped moving and glared at Chris.

"Turn that down! Turn that down. What time you have to be at work?" Chris demanded and asked.

Dontay turned the music off and replied, "I have to go in a minute."

Rico not knowing asked in a monotone voice, "Work where?"

"I got re-classed to be a porter in I-Cell house. I start today."

"Death row?" Rico uttered surprisingly.

"Yeah, it ain't nothing."

"You know you're going to get cold chills walking through there? You have the most deadliest, vicious, killers in that cell house. Monsters."

"I'm a killer, what you talking 'bout." Dontay imprudent just waved him off and got ready to leave. He was the leader out the three—all with little education. Before he left he stated, "If my girl call, tell her I will call her tonight when I get off of work. Don't be reckless with the phone either. I'll holler at ya'll later." Dontay referred to the cell phone he had. He strolled out the cell with a tough swagger.

"Open I-Cell house!" the guard shouted standing outside his booth area to the other officer.

Dontay stood behind his cleaning cart as the gate rolled open. He peered down the still range in thought of actually strolling down it. The shining white tile reflected the sunlight—the blue walls gave a sad feeling—and the black bars on every cell reminded him of a kennel.

Doom—clack! The range gate sounded when it fully opened.

Go, Dontay's conscious told him. He slowly pushed the cart onto the range in fear. His head shot back when he heard the gate closing. *I guess I'm trapped in here*, he thought.

He glanced down the huge tier of locked away killers. It was quiet—no sound, no movement. He could feel the men spirits floating around and they weren't even dead yet. The thought of death to come was avenging any time, any day. It sent prisoner's souls searching for God for forgiveness. The day of execution, the whole prison would go under silence for the convict put to rest.

Dontay got a cold chill and goose bumps rose upon his flesh. He thought about what Rico said, *you going to get cold chills walking through there, most deadliest, vicious, killers*. He grabbed the dust mop off the cart and slowly pushed it down the range.

"Kill me. Kill me," a whisper from a cell suggested.

Dontay stopped and looked back to see where it was coming from. He couldn't tell and he knew not to ever glance into another man's cell. He proceeded on.

After he was done sweeping, he mopped the tier. That was mostly his whole job. He couldn't pass or receive anything from the men on the range without the CO's approval.

At chow time, Dontay helped the officer with feeding. He placed the cups on every cuff board and filled them with kool-aid. That's when he made his first mistake. He took a glimpse into a man's cell. *The cell is huge, two times bigger than the average cell*, Dontay thought.

"What are you looking at?" the insane appearing white man grumbled and ran up to the bars. "What you want to see some dick!" Dontay froze with the pitcher of kool-aid in his hand. The man went to praying, "Ohh! What did I do Lord to deserve this. To suffer, starve, to die this way. My conscious is eating away at me like cancer. I can feel my skin peeling away. Oh God-odd! The pain is deep . . ."

Dontay stumbled away with the ewer of kool-aid. Mentally he felt he was feeding the living dead.

The officer watched from a distance and grinned as he put a tray in a slot.

When everyone received their meal, Dontay ate his food outside the tier in front of the guard's booth as he watched TV. After he was done eating, he picked up the trays then swept and mopped again.

The job was simple—clean, feed, watch TV, and the range stayed quiet from guys studying, reading, and learning everything that they could before they died.

After an intense day of work, Dontay headed back to his cell house.

Back at the cell, he got his cell phone from Chris and conversed with his girlfriend all night. The cell phone which was contraband was a pacifier and satisfied Dontay mentally.

The following week, Dontay picked up his money in commissary from the man they stumped half to death. The collection of soups, chips, and meats from debts and drug sales put a smile on his face and compelled him to enjoy the prison life. Commissary, drugs, money, mail, and phone time was the only things on his mind. He bagged up some heroin and dropped it off to a customer before heading to work. He was the man in his eyes.

"I-Cell house!" Dontay yelled with the dust mop in his hand to the officer in the booth. He was a pro at the job now he believed.

He slid through the gate before it rolled completely open and then began pushing the dust mop down the range as he rapped out loud.

"You look like the rest of the guys who want to stay here," pronounced a low granting voice from a cell.

Dontay stopped and waited to see if the man was talking to him. After a long pause, he asked, "What you say?"

"You heard what I said."

"No. I didn't catch it."

"Did I stutter?"

"I look like these other—"

"I knew you heard me." The voice gained strength as the man in the cell stayed in the shadows. "You look like the rest of the guys who want to stay here."

Dontay could tell the voice was coming from the cell behind him. He took four steps back and glanced into the cell. The man was in the dark staring right at Dontay. His eyes were bright and piercing. They locked eyes and sized each other up.

Dontay wanted to know why he said what he said and asked, "How I look like I want to stay here? Do you know me player?" He was offended by the comment.

The man slowly stepped out the shadows to his cell bars. His mid-size afro was uncombed, the grays in his beard stood out, his brown skin was clear and appeared smooth, and his well-built body showed in his tank top and black shorts. "Do you know where you're at?"

"Yeah, I-Cell house."

"I see you think shit's a game. You ever fought for your life?"

Dontay second guessed himself if the man could get out the cell. He wasn't any punk but at the same time, he wasn't ready to be fighting for his life. "What you mean?"

"Everyone here is fighting for their life or complaining to die. And you come through here pants sagging off your ass, rapping, disturbing my peace. I can't hear myself think. You're having too much fun. Have you exhausted all your remedies?"

"What remedies?" Dontay was bemused.

"You come through here rapping but don't know anything about the law. You go to trial or took a plea?"

He hesitated in thought of the decision he made and said, "A plea."

"You do a Post-Conviction Relief to try to overturn your conviction?"

"No, they say you can get more time by doing it, and they can pick up the charges that they dropped."

"Yeah, yeah, it all depends on the case. Don't let that thought render you. You have some serious time son?"

"I'm not your son, and yeah, I got twenty years."

"You want to go home?"

"Every day I wake up."

"You got any kids?"

"Yeah, a son."

"Who's there to protect him, show him how to grow into a man?"

"His mamma."

"You cool with that?"

"It is what it is for right now until I can mod out."

"You believe in the system that much they will modify you out?"

"I'm gonna pay a lawyer to get me out."

"You have any education about yourself, college, G.E.D., or in school now?"

"Naw," he said and shook his head. "None of them, don't need it to get money."

"What if you needed it to save your life, could you past the test?"

"Why you asking me this?"

His raspy voice turned aggressive as he gripped the bars and said, "I'm not here because I'm guilty of a crime . . . I'm here because I'm BLACK. Youngster, you better wake up before they have you in here for life. If you really wanted to go home, you would be in those books. Can you read?"

"What's that got to do with anything? Yeah I can read. Reading is not going to get me home."

"They wrongfully convict people every day. If you read your plea agreement then you would know—"

The guard walked on the deck and said, "Don't be making too much noise on this range." He didn't know what had transpired.

Dontay nodded at the officer and began pushing the dust mop. What the man had said went through one ear and out the other. *What do he know, he's on death row*, Dontay thought.

After work, Dontay met up with a customer and made a transaction in front of a lieutenant. The lieutenant saw the hand off and searched the two. He found the drugs on the customer and took both their names down.

That night, Dontay got into an argument with his girl-friend over the cell phone about him possibly receiving a conduct report. She made it a point to ask if he wanted to come home because they planned to try to modify his sentence and he couldn't afford any write ups, but he just made excuses in return.

Dontay thought about what the man on death row said as he went to sleep.

Dontay pushed the dust mop down the tier of I-Cell house in silence. When he came upon that man's cell, his raspy voice sounded out.

"Life is nothing but a copy of what it reflects. What you think, what you see, is how you react. Even though you have some originators, they still fall back to copying."

Dontay paused and took a step back. He glanced into the man's cell at him sitting at the big round table full of books. He didn't comprehend what the man said and added his own two cents, "Life is what you make it."

"True," he said. "So if you just sit there and let people take your life away, it's what you made it."

Dontay tilted his head and frowned in thought of what

he just said.

The man spoke again, "What's your name?"

"Tay. Dontay."

"Dontay, Terrence Booker. You can call me Mr. Booker. When you're ready to learn freedom, let me know."

Dontay took offense to what he said and approached the bars. "What you mean learn freedom? What you say is not going to get me free. You can't free your damn self."

"You're in a mental war and you not even prepared."

"I put guys on their backs in these cell houses. They don't want none of me."

"You may be strong physically, but mentally you're weak." Mr. Booker was cutting into Dontay's mind and he couldn't handle that. "I may be caged but I didn't lay down and I'm still fighting death."

Dontay felt the realness in his pain and remained silent.

"Have you ever been so lonely that you felt you was going to crumble and die from pain? Or set in a cell and had no one to talk too but your brain and waited for your number to pop up for your expiration date? No visits. No phone calls. They make shows about this but don't give you the real. They can't deliver the feelings that I feel. The pain that sleeps in my heart, that sets deep in my stomach, and engrossed in my mind. I'm in my cell twenty-four hours a day. Could you handle that? Could you handle a death sentence without hanging yourself?"

Dontay didn't know what to say, he just shook his head.

"I was just like you thought life was a game until I lost mines. But my mind didn't turn to acceptance like most guys that are locked up, it turned into a contender." Mr.

Booker cleared his throat. "Last week . . . I uhh . . . sent a clemency motion to the Parole Board . . . to remove this death sentence from me and give me life without the possibilities of parole, while I try to overturn my conviction." He coughed. "After my trial, I appealed my case with a lawyer all the way to the Supreme Court then I was left to fend for myself. I had to study day after day, night after night, to understand the language the courts used to fight with. I had papers scattered everywhere. I went prose in my petition to have my case heard again. They denied me on every stage all the way up to the United States Supreme Court. Now that they saw that, they want to give me the lethal injection. Here, I want to give you something that I had to learn, but it's up to you on how bad you want your freedom." Mr. Booker turned and stepped to his table, grabbed a book then brought it to the bars and stuck it out.

Dontay gave him a wondrous stare.

"They try to kill us mentally and physically. Look around you, this is far worse than any torture of the body. That's why you need to reach out. When you're ready for freedom you'll read this."

Dontay taking in what he said reached and grabbed it. It was a law book.

The CO came charging on the tier and shouted, "Hey! What's that he just handed you?" He grabbed the book out Dontay's hand.

"It's just a law book," Mr. Booker announced.

The officer flicked through it carefully to make sure any notes weren't being passed and informed, "You can't accept anything from them without going through me first.

Here you go. Next time I won't let you have it." He handed the book to Dontay then ordered, "Get back to work."

Dontay locked the book against the wooden stick and proceeded to sweep.

When his shift was over, he went to his cell and skimmed through the law book. He didn't know what to look for or where to start; he just saved some questions for Mr. Booker tomorrow.

"I bet if you went to your cell house and asked everyone if they went to trial or took a plea, ninety percent of them would say they took a plea," Mr. Booker verbalized. "And many of them took a plea under unconstitutional errors. And when you take a plea, you have to fight against that plea. You have to overcome the presumption of your guilt because you admitted it. You have to claim if it wasn't for your attorney's mistakes, you would have gone to trial. Or you have to find some type of unlawful error in your plea agreement, sentencing, or rights enumerated in the guilty plea statue at the time of your plea. So you have to go to the law library and send a motion to the courts for your plea and sentencing transcripts. Look through your transcripts, plea agreement, and paperwork thoroughly, and make sure it's in line with the statues of the law." He stuck out another law book. "This should help you."

The CO came trudging onto the range. "Hey! Hey!" the CO shouted. "What's that he just handed you?" He snatched the book out of Dontay's hands. "I told you, you couldn't receive anything from—"

"It's a law book!" Mr. Booker snapped at the top of his voice as he gripped the bars. "It's just a fuckin' law book!"

"Hey, hey, Mr. Booker, I'm just doing my job. Ease-zzy now." He didn't want to get the lifer upset because he knew he wouldn't have any problem snatching him into the bars and cutting his head off. He comforted the situation, "Next time you want to pass him something, just let me know first. I don't want my sergeant all up my ass. Here's the book back." He handed it back to Dontay without searching it. "We about to feed in a minute so get ready." He walked off.

Mr. Booker taking deep breaths directed his eyes towards Dontay and said, "I'm gonna let you get back to work. Remember, education is important. Don't wait until it's too late and pound your head with ifs. The world grows while you stay in the same position, same mind." He turned and stepped away from the bars. He never said goodbye because that's how he could leave, anytime.

Everyday Dontay would gain knowledge from Mr. Booker and was eager to learn more. The more he learned the more papers and books he had scattered over his room. He read something in the book Mr. Booker wrote that he enjoyed: *They take your youth away so you won't grow. Strip you from your family, friends, and all your possessions and don't give a damn if you have anything to survive on when you get out. You have to value your freedom and strive in the interest of justice.* Dontay made it a goal to seek his G.E.D. to open different avenues in his life and figured out what professional career he wanted to get into to bring home the money. He finally read his plea agreement thoroughly and found a possible error. He couldn't wait to see Mr. Booker.

"I can't fight against it because it's the law," Dontay explained to Mr. Booker.

Mr. Booker in disbelief gripped the bars and asked, "'Cause it's the law does it make it right?" His eyes penetrated Dontay waiting for an answer. From the long pause he persisted, "Was segregation in the early-mid 1900's okay? Was it okay when a white person got on the bus and the bus was full or packed and they didn't want to stand or go to the back of the bus, a black person had to get up?"

"No."

"It was the law. It had to be right. The law is nothing but another sinner's opinion that could be bias and wrong. Okay, let's go back a few years. The asperity of time you got for crack cocaine as opposed to powder cocaine. They were given blacks folks crazy time for crack cocaine and given white folks small time for powder cocaine. The asperity was challenged because it wasn't any difference between the two and it was ruled unconstitutional. What about mandatory minimum sentences? That got turned over because it was ruled unconstitutional. Then what about when the police were setting up road blocks for drunk drivers, but really was setting them up for drug searches. That was unconstitutional. It was the law to set up road blocks, but it wasn't the law to set up road blocks to conduct searches without any probable cause. They break the laws all the time, but it's okay for them because they work for the law. You're being judged by different type of criminals, unethical. The laws change all the time, so because it's the law does it mean its right? They're given men football jersey numbers for drugs, does that mean that's right?" He nodded his head down for an answer.

"No"

"They're making laws every day to entrap black people. When a law is extracted because it's ruled unconstitutional, they make another one. Check out the gun laws, they're taking young brotha's under. But it's cool to have one if you have a gun permit. And who goes out to get that? They're quick to take your rights from you so you can't be on the same level as them. If they can stay above you, they can control you and justify enslaving you. When you stop challenging the law, that's when it loses its effectiveness. The people who make the laws make them for their benefit. The penalties for crimes black people commit is more severe than the crimes white people commit. White people commit three times more crimes than black people, but three times more black people is in jail then white people. How is that? Look how they treat us in those court rooms. They jack up sentencing guide lines to make their job much easier by creating snitches to reduce their sentences. If it's such a crime, it should be one set sentence and not a wide range of time, in which a decision is made off of emotions and hidden beliefs. And the lawyers are bargaining right along with them, trading our freedom away. Brotha's fall every day, one day we will all stand tall in glory. When will we ever have a president like Nelson Mandela?"

"Probably never," Dontay answered. "Do you ever get to come out your cell?"

"When you enter here you're locked in until your time is up. And when I do they put me in dog chains."

Dontay took a real good look into his cell and realized this is not how he wanted to spend the rest of his life.

Certain things Mr. Booker said stuck with him.

"Crime has to stop at a whole, but everything is a crime . . . the jails are packed in America with all nationalities . . . their brain washing people to believe incarceration is the way . . . locking up the citizens doesn't make anything better . . . but what they're doing is creating more criminal minds to secure their jobs . . . it's an honor to give out a billion years to different people . . . their extending the path for their next generation to build on . . . at the same time, the same people who are convicting men and women is committing more crimes than them . . . think about how much stuff they got away with . . . racism still lies through America's justice system . . . Florida, Georgia, South Carolina . . . Texas . . . California . . . Indiana. . . . Look how they treat us in here . . . at least now you can feel how they felt on those slave ships . . . I was found guilty of a crime committed against white people . . . I had twelve white jurors, a white judge, prosecutor, and lawyer, and was found guilty with no evidence . . . how they gonna charge me with murder, robbery when they killed and stole a whole country . . . . they still celebrate thanksgiving don't they? I was convicted wrongfully . . . what you suppose to do when the whole circuit court is miscreant and acts in unity to cover up their oppression, change all your paper work to make you look guilty?" He dropped his head and made a weeping sound. "Fight! You have to fight. These muthafucka's aren't God. They're taking people lives away wrongfully. They're taking people lives away wrong-fully—"

EPILOGUE

A good impression can build
an everlasting fan base.

As the tour guide stepped through the crowd of visitors to Devon cell, he shouted, "Okay! That's enough. Enough of the prisons talk, we have to get going. We have a meeting to attend ladies and gentleman. All right, let's go, right this way." He directed the visitors with his arms wide to head for the core door.

The visitors began to turn away, but the nice looking lady hesitated and ogled at Devon with commitment. Devon wasn't the handsomest guy, but he was very impressive. He gazed into her eyes and phrased, "My name Devon Anderson. D.O.C. number, one, nine, two, one, nine, five."

She recited it silently moving her lips to let him know she had it and then gave a nod as she sauntered away.

Inside, Devon melted away. He got a burn of multiple feelings—the urge to be free. The way she switched her hips in them tight jeans, teased his emotions greatly. He wanted to hold her in his arms right then. He watched her until she disappeared. When he heard the core door close, he knew she was gone, but maybe not forever. *Damn, I didn't get her name*, he thought. For that short period of time, he didn't feel alone. He took a couple of steps and sat on his bed in thought of hearing from her.

Suddenly, the range grew loud from convicts commenting from cell to cell about the visitors. The visitors brought some excitement to their lives to talk about for an hour.

Boom, boom, boom, boom!

There was a knock on Devon's wall. Then his friend Bottom in the next cell shouted, "Anderson!"

Devon answered, "Yeah, what's up?" then arose and stepped to his cell bars.

"Damn, ol' girl was nice was-it she?"

"Yeah, she was a sight to see. She made my day."

"They were all in them stories. I heard you shout out your government and D.O.C. number. I'm like, look at him trying to come up."

"Sometimes you can make a connection from right here and it work out. That just motivated me to write some more."

"It would be nice if she wrote you. Maybe she could help you get your stories out there. When you getting back to writing?"

"I'm about to start right now. I will let you check out the story when I'm done."

"All right, get at me later."

Devon turned around and picked up the rest of his papers off the ground. He then sat at his desk and organized himself. He put on his headphones and turned on his MP3 player. He bobbed his head to the music and began to write.

As the world keeps turning, prison steady growing with no hopes of every stopping—and that's America for you— Iron bars and excuses—Judges, Prosecutors, and Lawyers bargaining on men, women, and kids' lives for favors and money reasons. So who's the real criminal?

The end for now

Tribute to Trayvon Martin

IN BEFORE SUNSET

I see myself dying every day before I walk out my house door.

See, I'm black, and live in America, where it's not safe for a young black male to walk the streets at night because he's profiled and viewed as a criminal.

So I better be in the house before sunset and stay put until sunrise. For the fact that, it's okay to murder us after you have harassed us and claim self-defense.

For the reason that, the community at trial will see that the killer is set free because blacks should be in before sunset.

Something's will never change. There's no equality in America.

Relax in Paradise

ACKNOWLEGMENTS

Spread me around the world
like a Bible . . .

It's 2:37a.m. I'm being held captive in this old, what
should be condemn, reddish brick building. It sucks. I can't
sleep because it's too cold. The weather outside is 15
degrees below zero, and this window I'm looking at is
cracked open. I can't close it because it's caged off. No one
can control the opening and closing of it except the prison
guards. I'm clothed in a pair of long johns, top and bottom,
two pair of socks, gray jogging pants, and a gray sweat
shirt. My doo rag holds down my dreads and my CL20
Koss headphones over laps that. I'm listening to
"Somebody loves you" by Plies. I'm coming down with
some sorter cold. My bones ache. A good hot bath right
now my body would appreciate. I'm so tired of taking
showers. Hold on . . . let me put on my state issued coat . . .
much warmer. This pen is froze to my hand, so all I have to
do is move my wrist, but it hurts to write, yet, I need to get
this out for America and the rest of the world. My desk is
filled with written on papers, books, and different kinds of
magazines. I got lucky tonight because it's quiet. Usually
it's a lot of endless motion and chatter. I've been sitting on
these stories for a while and should have been released
them, but I've been acting as my own attorney, so that

takes a lot of my focus away. Freedom is everything, and just wait until I can get to my own office space, I will be writing away like some of the bestselling authors. As you can vision, I write from experience of what goes on in prison and the pain that's felt behind bars. I witnessed so much corruption from the convict's and authorities. Overseer's that don't see any wrong in their wrong. So much goes on in here that it's safe to say: it's a different world. But I have met some very talented and cool people, as well as insane. This is a trying experience for me and every day I strive to help myself for the time out of my life that I can't get back. Luckily, I don't have any kids to stress about. I feel for the guys who do. Hopefully one day I will have some. But right now, I'm going to continue to write and bring a variety of things to read about or listen too. Let me get down to business with my appreciation on this project.

Thanks to the Most High for keeping me strong when I am weak. The discreet whispers with you have brightened my darkest days.

Thanks to the Authors who had the courage enough to write, that inspired me to write.

Uh oh, here she goes, Dianna. You stop me in mid-transition of writing a different book to write about jail/prison. Your words, 'You have to write about in there first.' Well, here you go. Special thanks for always picking up the phone when I call—for years. You've stayed down through the rain the sunshine is coming. For believing in me and helping me bring these stories to publication. Gratitude for the love and support.

My mother, thanks for the encouragement to keep

writing.

Uncle Joey, thanks for the push and efforts to promote this.

Anthony Smith, it's always a pleasure to work with you. Big thanks for putting your touches on this project.

Lauren, thanks for the support with my writing. The instant feedback on the stories and helping me spread the word. For staying strong through the adversity because you lost your job over corresponding with me, but didn't let that deterred you from continuing to encourage me to reach further.

Monica Courtney, for the compelling input after reading the stories, the cheer to keep writing, and the positive messages that you send. Hey Sista, don't let your writing go to waste, let it make money for you. I'm waiting to see that big motion picture with your name on it.

William a.k.a. Vision, for helping me stay focused and requesting my knowledge for growth. It helped me stay on top of my game. Don't be shy to make something of yourself.

Toby and Tyrone Grayson, thanks for the strength, encouragement, and talks about prison.

William Vanhorn, my brother from another color. You helped me out every way you could and given me strength to write at hard times. Thanks for your insight and input on the poem crash course of life. Continue to endure the struggle and keep fighting for freedom.

Guerilla War, thanks for your input and insight on life behind bars. You've been down 28 years, it's almost over.

Lorenzo, I always get a laugh when I talk with you and just think, you've been down 21 years and can still smile.

What can I complain about? Thanks for letting me know how rough it can get in those cell blocks.

Phillip Lee, just following you around could give me a lot to write about, always into something. Thanks for your input.

Miles, thanks for your insight and input on the poem "What a Letter Could Mean."

William Shaffer, thanks for going over a few of the stories and giving me your input.

Ms. Short, thanks for the help in my college writing class.

Lee, Lavelle, Sean, Taylor, and Janeen, for your teaching skills, proofreading, and encouragement.

Mrs. C, for the home cooked meals in Culinary Arts that kept me writing.

Da Beast, every day you gave me a boost to write, made me smile at difficult times, and sharpen my writing skills. Thanks so much.

Johnny B, I got your letters encouraging me to keep writing. Gratitude.

Keeasa, for checking in and spreading the word.

Abdul Hasan, for sending them kites to me and holding it down at Ross Correctional Institution. I'm waiting on your manuscript of That Street Life.

Alexis, Cheyenne, and Vonah, for staying down, the support and encouragement.

Lisa, thanks for the support up in Canada.

Arthur, thanks for staying down since we were kids. Write on.

John and Bolton, thanks for sharing writing techniques and feedback on the stories. Continue to write and make something of it.

Mr. Hayes, the big bull dozer is coming through. Thanks.

J. Bennett, Walters, and the yard dogs, Decker, Hoskins and Snyder, man give those guys back their contraband. Thanks for keeping it live from a guard's point of view.

2Savage, I look to see you on stage rocking the mic. Thanks for the lyrics at hard times.

2face, nothing can stop you but yourself. 6000 pushups straight, man that's amazing. Make your talent work for you. Thanks for the push.

Courtney a.k.a. Steven D-Bo-Ski, for sitting down and going over the Queen's English with me. You know it's hard to get around ones who understand. Keep writing and look for a better way.

Quincy Griffin, thanks for handling business and keeping ones in order.

Pork Skin a.k.a. Bright Wood. Thanks for keeping it live and giving me something to write about.

Susan H, for the smiles and encouragement to keep striving forward. Overall, it has run a long way. It helped me finish this and continue on. Thanks Suzie. Stay magnificent.

To the readers out there around the world, thanks for the support. I hope you enjoyed the tales from a jail cell. And to the young readers out there, who are constantly in trouble, change your direction so you won't have to experience the rough life of prison. Behind bars is not cool. Use your talents to make money for you. To the guys around me, Dreek, Mike Ford, Cadillac V, Goon, Dontel, TJ, Woogy, Kilo, Solomon, MarQuees, Nephew, Wanny, Baby D, Rosco, Pinky, Wild Wild, Booda, 64th, Pop, Murder, Keyshawn, Monster-the king of the jungle, Booie, JB, Lil Boo, Yates, Neal, PD, Mike Jones, Black, Toot, Dink a.k.a. on the deuce, Baby James, Vann-Bey, CC, Daleon, Jose, Tony Asaun, Chubbs, C, Real Black, Chuck, Joe Reed, D-Dex, Big Mac, Allan, Coke, Bronskey, Kalub, Jessie, No-No, Doobie, Big Bank Hank, Big T-post road, 2G, T-Man, LaDon, Fredie, Lomax, Bummy, El, Baby Lord, Dr. Eze, OG Al a.k.a The General representing Dirty World Records UGT Ent., Tucan, Eddie, Albert Hill, Chico, Luna, Castillo, Bird, Tez, John John, Gypsy, Wu, and the list just keeps going on. Plan and prepare for the best life ever. To the ones I have forgotten to list, don't take it personal. I'll just sign a book especially for you.

What you think is cool at an early age
You want find as cool at an older age
Wisdom will kick in
And God will become your friend

—Darvanni Autonomy

About the Author

Darvanni Autonomy is a native of Ohio. He is the Author of the inspiring novel Heat and Chemistry. As he goes through the asperity of incarceration, he shares his only freedom through his pen, in his words, what you read is what he sees.

Excerpt out of Book two
Tales From A Jail Cell
Department of Corrections

PROBATING

It's a physical world, where only
a few fight with their brains.

The judge slamming the gavel at his sentence hearing
notion through Michael Zachary's mind as he stared out the
window of the big blue bird bus shackled and handcuffed
next to another inmate on their way to a uniform life. The
growing sun beamed off the passing cars and trucks, as it
reflected off the windows and casted upon his pale facial
features. The scenery resembled causing boredom as they
went down the country roads. To him, everything seemed
to be passing him by. He knew this was his last ride for
some years and he couldn't even enjoy it. Missing summer
time fun with his girl was all he could think about.

As the bus pulled up to the facility, Michael peered at
the institution. The structure reminded him of project
buildings with busted out windows and rubbish scattered
over the grounds from the prisoners littering out the
windows.

When the bus came to a halt, one of the transporting
guards announced, "Ladies! We reached the gladiator's
dome. Some of ya'll go need protection, let me know now.
If you scared, stay your ass on the bus. For the guys that
are not on their first rodeo, better let these newcomers
know how things work around here. Well, good luck at the

State Farm." The officers' stepped off the bus and locked their weapons away as the bus was searched by the station guard at the post to enter through the prison's gates.

The recidivist felon next to Michael commented as he nodded his head, "Yeah, yeah, it goes down here. You can't be scared. You have to come in and take the first initiation. Anybody talks crazy, you have to hit'em right in the mouth, if not, the goons are going to come see you."

Michael looked at him and didn't say anything. Butterflies began to swim in his stomach. *This is much different from the county jail—more dangerous*, he imagined.

The recidivist felon spoke again, "This your first time?"

Michael cleared his throat nervously and replied, "Yes."

"You apart of any gangs?"

"No."

"It's a lot of gang activity here, and if you're not a part of anything, mind your business or you will get fucked over. They are going to come for you to join. It's up to you to be a man or not."

"So are we going to be in two man cells?" All Michael could collected in his mind of prison was what he saw off the TV show Lock up Raw, the county jail, and the Reception Diagnostic Center where they just came from.

"No, it's dormitories here. A bunch of criminals stuffed inside large rooms. Anything can happen at any minute. Not like in the cells where you're locked down and safe at night."

The bus started up and slowly rolled to receiving. Michael was curious and wanted to know more, he asked, "So it's a lot of beds lined up in the dorms?"

"You'll see. How much time you got?"

"Two and an half years."

"Watch who you fuck wit, they will have you in some bullshit." The bus stopped. It was time. The guard opened the front gated door. Everyone stood then followed single file off the bus and into the brick building. The small storage looking setting made Michael feel unwelcomed. He read the sign posted high on the storage cage: *Be seated and remain quiet.*

The transporting guard stepped in and unshackled everyone. He instructed for them to strip out of their orange jump suits and shower shoes and put it inside the garbage bag so he could go on his next destination.

One of the guys clutching his stomach struck off running for the toilet that sat behind a three foot brick wall to relieve himself because he was terrified inside. With his next move, he didn't get to make it to general population, he immediately checked in.

After receiving their khaki pants, khaki shirts, brown State boots, combination lock, radio, bedding, property box, and sack lunch, they were escorted to the orientation dorm—17 south.

On their way past 17 north, the punks of the institution stood in the windows and greeted them with effeminate mannerism as they waved, "Hey boys! Welcome to prison! Head for five dollars!"

Michael's eyes bulged when he saw the girlish men in the windows waving. Some of the guys couldn't do any-thing but laugh as they kept walking.

When they entered 17 south carrying their gray boxes, Michael's head drew back. The first guy he saw had two black eyes. He was alarmed—it was hell to come. His eyes examined the place. It was two sides of the dorm—C and D—75 beds on each side. Majority of the men were running around playfully and it was very load—TV area, poker table, and bed area.

"Sit your stuff down right there and come over here so I can write your names down and give you your assigned bed," the dorm officer standing at the podium next to the door said to all the newcomers as he pointed and then moved to close the door.

They did so and walked over. A few of them dropped their boxes making a thunderous sound. It made Michael jump. He looked at the frail dorky CO and thought, *what the hell is he going to do if something brakes out—nothing.*

The guard began to look at ID's then gave out bed numbers. After Michael received his bed number, he picked up his box and went searching for it until he found it—33 D. He walked up and stared at the white plastic mat that was on the metal bed frame. He wondered if they were serious that he had to sleep on a foot and an half wide mat. You couldn't turn over by the looks of it. But he looked around and saw everyone else had one. Instantly he hated it. He made his bed then flopped down on it. He ate his two cold cut sandwiches and orange out his sack lunch as he observed the dorm. It was pretty hot so his eyes searched for an air unit, but he only found fans at the end of each cube's wall. He couldn't believe there wasn't any AC.

One of the guys who came in with him walked over and asked, "Hey man, you want to play some Dad?"

Dad was a card game a lot of guys played. Michael glanced up at the guy standing over him and replied, "No, I don't know how to play." He declined the offer because he wasn't ready to mix in with the other men. He wanted to avoid confrontation as much as possible. He just relaxed back on his mat and stared up at the florescence lights.

3 p.m. rolled around and the CO yelled out, "Line up for chow!"

Michael couldn't believe they had to eat dinner so early. With no commissary, he knew he would be starving tonight. He got himself together and headed out in orderly fashion. They didn't have to go far because the chow hall was right next door. Going outside gave a refreshing feel, but when Michael walked into the north side prisoner's dining room, he turned his nose up along with every other inmate.

"It smells like animal piss and diced onions!" an inmate shouted.

Michael waved his hand in front of his face as he examined the dining hall. Seven rows of rectangular steel tables filled the room, the L-path to the two pick up windows was directed by a yellow guard rail, the big yellow fans mounted on the walls blew hot air, and the six orange drink coolers sat on its own individual racks on top of a steel table along the wall. The inmate kitchen workers were lined up against the wall with their push brooms in hand, and the officers were positioned throughout the dining hall to assist with feeding. A baby bird flew from pipe chase to pipe chase trying to figure a way back outside.

"There goes a bird," guys uttered astonishingly as they pointed.

Michael followed in line and grabbed his tray and filled his small cup with juice then sat in row four as the CO instructed. The food appeared horrible to Michael's eye sight. America Goulash was the main course meal. But the guys in 17 south didn't care what it was because they were starving.

The dining hall began to grow loud as it filled to its capacity with prisoners. The officers began to pester the inmates to rush to eat as the kitchen workers pushed their brooms in each aisle.

Michael tried to stomach the food as fast as he could. He glimpsed the guys at his table as he listened to different conversations going on around him.

Boldly, one of the kitchen workers eased up to Michael's table and whacked the white guy sitting next to Michael right in the head with a lock in the sock. The blow was fracturing and sounding. The man let out a small cry as he cringed up.

Blood squirted over the trays.

The whole table jumped up as the gang member disguised as a kitchen worker continued to pound the man's skull.

74272522R00106

Made in the USA
Middletown, DE
22 May 2018